Rivers of Ink

Literary Reflections on the Penobscot

Edited by Steven Long

Introduction by Sherri Mitchell Weh'na Ha'mu Kwasset

Cover Design: Heather Magee | www.hmagee.com
Book Design: Mariella Travis | www.alleiram.com
Map Illustration: Dan Kirchoff | www.dankirchoff.com

ISBN
978-1-961905-03-0 (Paperback)
978-1-961905-02-3 (eBook)

12 Willows Press
Winterport, Maine
www.12willowspress.com

Table of Contents

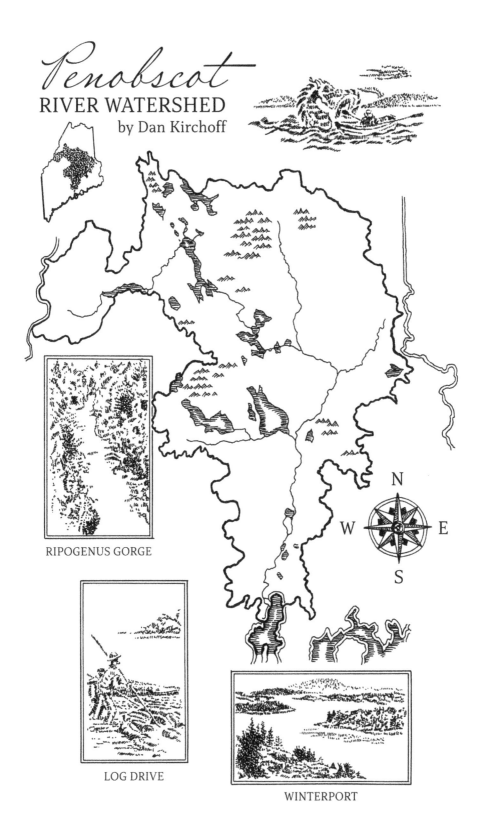

Penobscot
RIVER WATERSHED
by Dan Kirchoff

RIPOGENUS GORGE

LOG DRIVE

WINTERPORT

N
W   E
S

Acknowledgments

Some of the works in this collection were previously published in the following:

"Nine Ways to Get to Bangor" by Linda Buckmaster in her collection *Heart Song and Other Legacies* (Huntress Press, 2007)

"The Same Stream Twice" by Valerie Campbell is an excerpt from her novel *Same Stream Twice*

"The Mystery of 'Bagaduse' and the Penobscot Watershed's Monsters" by Loren Coleman is an adaptation, expansion, and enhancement of a note in his book *The Monsters of Massachusetts: Mystery Creatures of the Bay State* (Stackpole Books, 2013)

"A Day in the Life of a River Driver" by Mary Morton Cowan in her book *Timberrr ... A History of Logging in New England* (Millbrook Press, 2003)

"Scripture" by Kara Douglas in the *Frost Meadow Review,* vol. 3 (Spring/ Summer 2019)

"Narrow River to the North" and "Watershed Haibun" by Kathleen Ellis in her collection *Narrow River to the North* (Maine Authors Publishing, 2011)

"Full Chorus" by Jean Anne Feldeisen in her collection *Not All Are Weeping* (Main Street Rag Publishing, 2023)

"I Wish I Could Describe Winter Sky in Maine" by Jean Anne Feldeisen in the self-published collection *Catching Fireflies* (2023) by Jean Anne Feldeisen and Argy Nestor

"Once Again, the River Runs Wild" by Robert Klose in *The Christian Science Monitor Weekly* (May 8, 2017)

"Polar Vortex" by Hans Krichels in his collection *We Have Met the Enemy* (Maine Authors Publishing, 2021)

"Deep in the Forest" and "The Forest, It Lay Bare Now" by "Twinkle" Marie Manning in her collection *Accompanied* (Matrika Press, 2021)

"Into the Forest" by Meadow Rue Merrill is an excerpt from her novel *The After Forest*

"Great Blue" by Leslie Moore in *Spire: The Maine Journal of Conservation and Sustainability* (2023)

"Lucky Streak" and "Wild Song" by Leslie Moore in her collection *Grackledom: Poetry, Prints, and Drawings* (Littoral Books, 2023)

"Law of Conservation of Bobbi" by Gary Rainford in his collection *Adrift: The Love and Loss of Living with Dementia* (North Country Press, 2022)

"Restoration" by Patricia Smith Ranzoni in *The Catch,* no. 12, vol. 1 (2013)

"Welcome to the Penobscot, Pajaro Jai/Enchanted Bird" by Patricia Smith Ranzoni in the *Blue Ocean Institute's Sea Stories* (2007)

"Liquidation" by Karin Spitfire in her collection *The Body in Late Stage Capitalism* (Illuminated Sea Press, 2021)

Editor's Note

STEVEN LONG

The Penobscot River watershed covers over 8,500 square miles of Maine forestland. Called Pαnawάhpskewi by its namesake people, it means "where the white rocks extend out." This name references the river's widening near Bucksport and Orland before it empties into Penobscot Bay.

Beyond the four major branches that form the upper Penobscot, a dense network of approximately 1,200 lakes and ponds and 180 rivers and streams drains into a meandering 240-mile-long river. This is the mighty Penobscot.

Given recent global weather events, the Penobscot is a fitting theme for *Rivers of Ink: Literary Reflections on the Penobscot*, the anthology for this year's Bangor Authors' Book Fair & Literary Festival. All profits from this anthology will be donated to the Friends of Katahdin Woods and Waters' fundraising campaign, A Monumental Welcome, which supports the construction of a visitor contact station, priority park projects, and Wabanaki-directed projects.

Just as the Penobscot draws strength from countless bodies of water, this anthology gains power from exceptional writing and behind-the-scenes support, without which *Rivers of Ink* could not have come together in only six months' time—a remarkable achievement. My gratitude to Sherri Mitchell Weh'na Ha'mu Kwasset for the introduction, Annaliese Jakimides for editing, Jennifer Nelson Simpson for social media scheduling, Heather Magee for the cover, Dan Kirchoff for the map, and Mariella Travis for the interior design.

Thanks to the Bangor Greendrinks, Bangor Public Library, and Friends of Katahdin Woods and Waters for marketing help. And thanks also to Christopher Packard, the book fair's director. He asked if I wanted to produce an anthology, and I said "Yes!" without hesitation.

My wife and I moved from Chicago to Stockton Springs more than two decades ago. I still remember how breathtaking the view was. Like my first view of the Penobscot, this anthology has impacted me on many levels. I hope it does the same for you.

Introduction

SHERRI MITCHELL WEH'NA HA'MU KWASSET

Currents of Connection

I was born Pɑnawɑ́hpskewi[1] and raised on an island nation surrounded by the Penobscot River. We are closely related, the river and me. She is the first citizen recorded on our tribal census, an acknowledgment that we all draw our lives from her waters.

My grandfather introduced me to the river at a very young age. It was in her waters that I first learned of my place within creation and where I came to understand our people's deep connection to that entire riverine system. While floating on those waters, my grandfather taught me respect by showing me how to paddle a canoe without disturbing the water. I remember watching him paddle and noticing tenderness in his movement. A type of tenderness that was not rooted in gentleness or affection but was instead an expression of reverence. The kind of reverence that is tipped with awe, the sort that humbly acknowledges when you are in contact with a presence greater than the self. It is an experience of one soul touching another. This type of connection has an inexplicable vitality that remains long after the contact has ended. Even the slightest touch, when imbued with real tenderness, can be felt upon the skin for a lifetime. This tenderness keeps the touch of the water lingering on our skin and imbues the memory of us, as Pɑnawɑ́hpskewi, into the water. It is this that characterizes our relationship with one another.

Our traditional way of life, *skejinawe bamousawakon*, is measured through a network of balanced relationships that are highlighted in our cultural value system, specifically in the phrase *Psilde N'dilnabamuk*, which means "I offer this for all my relations." On the surface, this phrase recognizes our interrelatedness with all life. When you look deeper, you realize that it is an awareness that our thoughts, words, and actions have a profound impact on the entire living world. This is why we end

---

1   Pɑnawɑ́hpskewie, a citizen of the Penobscot Tribal Nation.

our public statements, prayers, and requests with these words, to keep us mindful of the relationships woven around us and remind us of our responsibility toward all our relatives, human and nonhuman alike. For more than 500 generations (15,000 years), our people have maintained relationships with the plants and animals in and along the river, relying on them for food, medicine, ceremony, and well-being. Over the last few centuries, there have been many attempts to unsettle these relationships and to displace us from our home along the river, but we remain.

Changing Waters

In the 1600s, industrial activity came to Wabanaki territory in the form of logging. By 1832, Bangor, Maine, was the world's largest shipping port for lumber.[2] The first paper mill in the state began operating in 1734 along the Presumpscot River.[3] Before long, there were paper mills on rivers across the state, including our beloved Penobscot. Four paper mills have operated along the river during my lifetime. The pollution from these mills disrupted vital ecosystems that supported species integral to our cultural survival. For example, decades of industrial pollution and damming brought the Atlantic salmon and other anadromous fish near extinction. Butch Phillips, a Penobscot elder, calls these fish the refugees of the river, forcibly removed from their Indigenous habitat by industrial misbehavior.

Maine waters are the last cold-water refuge to anadromous fish in the United States. Warming in these waters is a threat to fisheries throughout the Northeast. Sadly, fisheries are not the only habitat being impacted. Warming trends along the river have also dramatically reduced moose populations by causing unprecedented growth in winter tick activity. This has resulted in massive die-offs in young moose and significantly decreased adult reproductive rates. A 2018 study showed that approximately 70 percent of the moose calves born in our territory were killed by winter tick disease.[4]

---

2   The Maine Highlands. "Natural Wonders Endless Discovery: Lumbering in Maine," in *The Maine Highlands Guidebook*. November 2023. https://themainehighlands.com/

3   University of Maine, Pulp + Paper Foundation. "A Brief History of the Industry." November 2023. https://umaineppf.org/2021/01/08/a-brief-history-of-the-industry/

4   H. Jones, P. Pekins, L. Kantar, I. Sidor, D. Ellingwood, A. Lichtenwalner, and M. O'Neal. "Mortality Assessment of Moose (Alces alces) Calves during Successive Years of Winter Tick Epizootics in New Hampshire and Maine." *Canadian Journal of Zoology*, vol. 97, no. 1 (January 2019).

Another danger posed by warming water temperatures is the increased occurrence of algal blooms. The U.S. Environmental Protection Agency has warned that increased freshwater temperatures leads to more algal blooms.[5] Freshwater algal blooms are hazardous to fish, other animals, and humans. They contaminate drinking water, destroy habitat, and pose real threats to human and animal lives. There are three main types of toxins associated with algal blooms: neurotoxins, which cause a series of neurological conditions; hepatotoxins, which cause damage to the liver; and dermatoxins, which cause skin and respiratory issues.[6]

During my childhood, swimming and eating fish from the river was forbidden in my family because of these toxins and other carcinogenic compounds that my grandfather feared were in the water. The justification for his fears was often seen on the bodies of those who swam in the river, in the form of sores that dotted their arms and legs.

More than any other factor, the warming of our waters caused by industrial pollution has disrupted our relationship with the river. It has interfered with the continuity of our cultural and traditional practices and increased the incidence of environmental illness among our people, creating genuine threats to our survival as Pαnawáhpskewi.

Standing with the River

In response to the dire threats posed by industrial pollution, John Banks, the natural resources director of the Penobscot Nation, went on a mission to hold industry accountable for the harm it was causing the Penobscot River.

John began working for the Tribe in 1980 and immediately took the lead on addressing contaminants within the river. In the 1990s, the U.S. Department of the Interior, acting on behalf of the Penobscot Nation, began a natural resources damages proceeding against Lincoln Pulp and Paper (LPP). In 1999, the Bureau of Indian Affairs issued "Final Report: The Economic Value of Foregone Cultural Use: A Case Study of the Penobscot Nation." The bureau found that the Penobscot Nation had been denied its rightful relationship with the Penobscot River and estimated the natural resource damages to be somewhere between $32 million and $64 million. Following the release of this report, LPP was forced to

---

5   U.S. Environmental Protection Agency. "Climate Impacts on Water Quality." February 22, 2023. https://www.epa.gov/arc-x/climate-impacts-water-quality

6   Melissa Denchak. "Algal Blooms 101." Natural Resources Defense Council, August 28, 2019. https://www.nrdc.org/stories/freshwater-harmful-algal-blooms-101

rebuild its bleach plant at a cost of nearly $100 million, driving it into Chapter 11 bankruptcy and, ultimately, out of business. As of this writing, no paper companies are discharging into the Penobscot River.

Meanwhile, the Tribe spent over thirty years actively building strong ally networks up and down the river with local municipalities, federal agencies, environmental organizations, and energy companies. This work resulted in the creation of the Penobscot River Restoration Project, a unique collaboration between the Penobscot Nation, seven conservation organizations, the State of Maine, the federal government, and, surprisingly, a power company. This group's work led to the removal of the two dams on the lower Penobscot and the improvement of fish runs at several other dams.

The outcomes have been staggering. In 2022, nearly a decade after the removal of the dams, the Maine Department of Marine Resources reported the largest run of river herring ever recorded on the Penobscot River.[7] It also noted that the Atlantic salmon population had doubled from the previous year, making it the second-highest recorded salmon run within the last decade.

Today, the river faces new challenges, and protecting and improving the ecological integrity of her waters now rests on a new generation of Panawáhpskewi. My greatest hope is that over the next two generations, we will once again learn how to move along the river in the ways that our ancestors did without disturbing the water.

The essays and poems contained in this book illustrate the same love and tenderness that my grandfather expressed in his relationship with the river. They tell of the many ways that rivers flow through and shape the lives of all those they touch. And if you look closely, you may see that the touch of the water remains on the authors' skin.

Psilde N'dilnabamuk—I offer these words for all my relations.
Sherri Mitchell Weh'na Ha'mu Kwasset, Penobscot Nation
November 2023

---

7   Susan Sharon. "Strong River Herring, Atlantic Salmon Runs Observed in Penobscot River." Maine Public, December 1, 2022. https://www.mainepublic.org/environment-and-outdoors/2022-12-01/strong-river-herring-atlantic-salmon-runs-observed-in-penobscot-river

Liquidation

Karin Spitfire

For 36 years I've slept on some shore of Penobscot bay, paddle the
east and west branches of the Penobscot river, transverse
Penobscot county to get to medway, lincoln, the golden road, visit
Penobscot marine museum, Penobscot theater company, read
Penobscot pilot, smell the Penobscot potato factory, wake up to the
weather on bay

Penobscot river watershed covers 8,750 square miles from
bucksport to the canadian/maine border extends with some easy
portages to the Allagash into the st. john all the way to new
brunswick or over to the Kennebec down to popham and the bay,
from the bay you can get anywhere, Schoodic, Monhegan

I know a few of the carrying places, can read the waters some
know where I might find wild berries, sight eagles, great blue
heron, from castine to isle au haut, brooklin to camden hills, belfast
to mt. desert, know where I might go swimming, Megunticook,
Pemaquid, Naskaeg names I have learned to say the settlers' way,
but none we appropriate like Penobscot.

a mispronunciation of the people's name for themselves, the river,
the land, Pαnawάhpskewi, meaning the river the land the people

here for some 13,000 years, 90% annihilated by incoming
immigrant germs, the remaining estimate of 10,000 in 1700, fought
with the colonists in their revolution, now number under 2,000, cut
down by genocidal scalp bounties, war, alcohol, child abduction

The Penobscot treated into 22 square acres of their home land, a
swath of the river and its islands from medway to old town now
the state that dubs itself maine claims this stretch, the river, does
not include the water.

Pαnawάhpskewi Land, Pαnawάhpskewi River, Pαnawάhpskewi People.

Our Once and Future River

PAUL A. LIEBOW, MD

In olden days the Penobscot was a waking dream
of coral reef abundance and diversity.
Vast spring migrations of riverine life mirrored
the plaintive honkings of ducks and Canada geese overhead.

Salmon magically returning from Greenland and Icelandic seas
spawned in silence and privacy all the way up
from the Narramissic River, Marsh Stream,
and Sunkhaze Meadows to shady groves near Canada.

Uncountable alewives surged silver in full flower moonlight,
while a billion tiny elvers set out to find their way
home from the sinking vortex of the Sargasso Sea
where their parents had set their eggs adrift.

Huge stripers cavorted well up beyond Bangor,
two million shad played in the bright waters of May,
and pink petals of shadblow floated on the wind—
spring plum blossoms from ancient Chinese poetry.

Prehistoric ten-foot sturgeon cruised the depths
of the lower channel on red October days,
so powerful that Winterport sports had themselves
towed around like whalers on a "Nantucket sleigh ride."

Then for several neglectful generations, the river choked
and steamed brown—a stinking cadaver of industrial shame.
Mercury and chemicals, dams and the politics of greed
killed so many noble creatures from The Maker's Dominion.

A log pond smirked down by the mill in Bucksport
where people snickered and winked or sighed
about what was permitted to seep or be thrown in—
but never dared let their kids swim in the water.

I vividly remember the Great Green Bridge to Verona
from my childhood on the way Downeast to Gramp's
but too few would look beneath its swirling tides or into
the secrets of its hidden heart, deep in the Great North Woods.

Now all our dignity and hard work have been sold overseas,
the grumbly old mill, that gave our town its life,
is a huge pile of scrap metal and weeping cement,
and we struggle once more to find our future in the river.

But the river does smile up again, at a new Great Gray Bridge,
whose Maine granite sings in the eternal flames of JFK,
sways with the lines of the Washington Monument—
and sleeps in winter-camp with our soldiers in Fort Knox.

Its towers look back down to Mosquito Mountain and Waldo,
out on Katahdin's shimmering cerulean blue northers,
the sun's golden lily pad cupping the islands of the bay,
the fish and their river returning home to the Penobscot people,
the People of the Dawn, because so many care.

Reflections on the Water

*As exhibited on the interpretive panels on the Bucksport
waterfront at the mouth of the Penobscot River*

Wherever on Earth fresh water joins salt the people come
in promise and praise, as here where this ancient power flows
without end. Here by the mouth and voice of Mayne's greatest
watershed on its race by Katahdin mountain down to this Bay.
Only Here. This Penobscot Place. This Ancestral Presence
with our descendant eagles, salmon and sturgeon restored
in eternal re-Creation. These visions. These birchbark canoes.
These countless ocean-going vessels again. You. Here. Your heart
riding the tide. This Now. This Tomorrow.
    Oh you of this timeless Passage, return!

I Saw an Eagle Die Today

JEAN ANNE FELDEISEN

Yesterday he stood tall
on the rocky ledge
        overlooking Cobscook Bay
body arched neck strong
leaning into space.

His head tilted toward the water,
turned deliberately, first one side
        then the other, alert
for shadow of fish
        far below in the tide.

Today, an unnatural
pose. Not a bird—
        A tortured dancer
head strains to the sky,
neck extended, legs stiff
wings stretched
                wide enough to touch
        the two   electric wires.

Then
        falls

Head
        over feet
                over head
and thumps
                Hard

onto the pavement
in my gut.

South Turner Mountain

MATT BERNIER

We told ourselves we could turn back anytime.

Gazing from the wooded shore of Sandy Stream Pond,
the bare rock summit of South Turner Mountain
looked like the ruins of a temple;

three thousand one hundred and twenty-two feet
above sea level some deity had built a temple
only to see it destroyed by weather,

and in that moment we decided to become pilgrims,
to leave a Zen garden of sandy shallows, rippled water,
boulders and yellow birches

and ascend one thousand feet in zero point two miles,
twisting and squeezing between rows of boulders
as though exiting crowded pews,

chorus of black-throated green warblers singing amens
as a hermit thrush beckoned us to higher realms,
golden-crowned kinglets chirping reverently

as we neared a side trail to a spring, a holy site,
burbling out of the bare rock like a miracle
as a toad hopped across our path

hoping to find a cure for its leprous appearance,
or maybe just seeking baptism over and over
in the church of its amphibious youth,

so we climbed higher and higher into thinning air,
mountain cranberries leading us to tree line,
to gardens of bonsai potted in gravel,

and we gaped, looking up at the ruined temple,
still gilded with sunshine even as shifting spirits
darkened and clouded Katahdin,

my partner waiting amidst the stunted spruces
as I continued my journey onward and upward,
the vulnerable meeting the venerable,

stepping through the temple's granite stones,
blue blazes punctuating the irregular path
like blasphemous curses,

until I looked down at distant Sandy Stream Pond
where a moose hunched like a priest in dark robes,
plume of silt wafting behind like incense,

and I descended quickly, weak kneed in my rebirth,
destined thereafter to climb and declimb mountains
seeking enlightenment,

and further down the slope a lone wood frog,
shimmering in silky green and black monk's robe,
crossed our unsteady path,

so high in elevation it would have to begin its journey
down the mountain before autumn deepened,
before reincarnation began,

and back at Sandy Stream Pond the priestly moose
had disappeared like a savior into the wilderness,
so we looked away, then looked at ourselves.

Law of Conservation of Bobbi

GARY RAINFORD

Denise, a med-tech who will quit
next Wednesday because Memory Care
is a revolving door of turnover and

hardship, plungers a dose of liquid
Ativan into Bobbi's mouth, lips shaking,
hands shaking, shoulders shaking

as if gale force winds rush alongside
the rushing of blood in her veins, 41 knots
of flesh, bones, and primal confusion

in her brown, twitchy eyes. "Do you
have pain?" I put my hand over Bobbi's
thin, arthritic hand. "I want out," she

mutters, and I imagine her diaphanous
soul separating from her decrepit material
form, rising to the florescent lights

and sailing across the common room,
through the walls, into the trees where it
continues to rise and expand, wispy

fragmented energy transferring into the
warm, yellow, March sun patrolling over
the frozen Penobscot River in Bangor.

Deep in the Forest

"TWINKLE" MARIE MANNING

Deep in the forest,
Quiet shapes the sound of immense emollient twilight.
Saturated shades of perpetual green caress the sky.
Blues sink down to violet.
Leaves land lightly;
      Layering lanes to linger upon.
Seekers of silence satisfied,
Within this modulating animated tenement.
Sanctuary of Solace found beneath copious canopies of trees;
Living, breathing.

Rocky River, High Water

Doug Barrett

When I awake the first thing I hear is the river
roaring over the rocks above the bend.
              The rocky river
never silenced at the highest water
washing down from garden beds wood eroded from the Veazie Mill
          washing up bricks and river-rock stepping stones
aerating, cleaning itself
          flushing chemicals to the sea blue black white
creator provider destroyer, its pure
conversation rhythms indistinguishable from noise.

Spring cormorant reverse river dark gray birds
flying and fishing their way upstream in threes and fours
          day   after day.
Summer song sparrow trilling
          so loud
as to almost drown the river out
osprey fish dive
                              eagles in their spy tree
all these silences   of the roaring river.

Two rivers: artery pulsing out timber and furs
vein sucking blood inward toward the heart
                    alcohol guns smallpox
atmosphere ghost-humid:
moose, deer, porcupines, Panawáhpskewi, mill girls, port girls
          river-lured

momentary flicker at the top of the stairs.

Always something wrong but
        what can straighten out water?
Embraced by fish nets
        street grids, spider webs
                thoughts, plans, prayers
measured by mathematicians
        dams pure resistance now gone
salmon follow cormorant conduit
        bucking the current of easy living.

Walking up Pump House Road from the dam site
        sandpiper
proceeding ahead of me through the woods
where rain has made rivulets in the dirt road.
Hey there, what are you doing back here in the woods?
        At every step it bobs its butt
slowly twerking to unheard music
        and now roadside grass rustling.
        What's *that*?
Another bird—spotted, fluffy ... twerking too ... its chick.
Pecking and bobbing uphill downstream
        flowing in parallel channel
shoreline haunts submerged.

At night the last thing I hear is the river's monotone music
flooding the swimming holes, washing seaward all but
        the ghosts
sweeping off ego superego and id   language culture   nature itself
not by water   but by water's voice   its spirit.
"Do you hear it," said Xuansha, "the sound of the roaring river?
Enter there."
                Into what?

Nine Ways to Get to Bangor

LINDA BUCKMASTER

One watershed: Penobscot Bay gathering,
funneling every rill and stream, from its namesake
running past the hospital to the waters at the end
of my street. Carry on—Marsh Stream, Goose River,
Meadow Brook, Kenduskeag, Westcott Stream, Hurds Pond,
Mendall Marsh, Passagassawakeag, Burnt Swamp,
Belfast Harbor.

Three surgeries: Biopsy, lymph node, lumpectomy, Route 1,
1A, 141, 139, 69, Dahlia Farm Road, City Point,
Head of the Tide, Oak Hill, Nealey's Corner, Exit 49.

Four hospitals: Waldo County, Pen Bay, St. Joe's, Eastern
Maine, osprey, porcupine, scrub jay, road kill, pothole, lesser newt.

One diagnosis: Prospect, Frankfort, Waldo, Stockton Springs,
Belfast, CancerCare, Winterport, Searsport, Monroe, Hampden, bald eagle.

Seven weeks of radiation: Exxon, Irving, Mobil, Coke for the good
things in life, two hot dogs for a dollar, Dino's Pizza, general store,
road work, free zucchini, real estate real estate real estate, blind drive.
Five years of follow-up: Gowned waiting.

Twenty seasons on the Penobscot:
Freeze up,
ice out,
spring flood, carry on.
Skunk cabbage, fiddlehead, shad bush, trillium, skullcap,
fireweed, goldenrod, swampberry, hackmatack, fir.

Twenty thousand years ago: Ice pack weighing
heavy on earth's crust. Glacier thaw receding, lifting,
leaving behind rock
rubble, limestone drift,
granite ledge and groundwater
moving unseen below, squeezing
between cracks, through soil to
          run and rise and fall again.

One watershed:
Carry on.
Carry on.

Yin and Yang, at Morse Cove

James Brasfield

Morning mist lifts
to brightness, and I'm *in* it, and it in me,
a slow embodiment of the mind's eye
from presence gathering

the ocean tide coming in,
the river from the mountains,
the creek flowing from woods—
the currents find their way
to one rhythm lapping.

A cormorant bobs on the swells,
diving to find, to overtake,
to bring to light, as when my own steps
will be what my future held.

*

Stones, lodged in the wet sand,
surrender their sheen a tide will return,

and holding her shoulders, a swimmer
stepping into water

and a shell gatherer standing still

gaze up at the calls of birds arriving,

and hear their sudden wings
close overhead.

*

How daylight expands from night fading,
how daylight withdraws in the tidal dark ...

Moon-driven, with or without
the wind's push over mountains and deserts

under the sea—what will waves bring
and take with their reports?

—Stones (polished, four tides each day),
their siblings yet to surface,

a tree and a bird flag a memory.

*

Suddenly within a feeling I have lived
this instance
of morning once before ...

I remember a midsummer birch,
starlings foraging among
dandelions, that day

in this moment: waves
rising to this calm morning,
supersonic the flight of moments—

the seconds measured: how long
can that cormorant stay underwater ...
now till then, a bit of trust,

its breath, then water dripping from its feathers.

on blue rushing river

LISA PANEPINTO

ancient body
lined with cedar
pines and oak

saying a wish
for happiness
and no suffering
for anyone
made of her
star water
deserving care

coyote loons owl
being themselves
singing wildly

fish jumping
cleansing the channels

cormorants riding
the eddies
my kin

singing rock me
on the water

taking bottles out
of waves
returning butterflies

floating under bridges
atop a boat

hawks shining
from beach wood shore
the guiding light

scent of juniper
washing the stones
making all new

from the depths
of unseen spring
coming to a holy place

Follow the River Home

CHRIS DAVIS

I was little. My younger brother Stephen was even littler. During the summer between my first- and second-grade years at Abraham Lincoln Elementary School, my Grammy Butcher cared for us while our parents were at work. We spent our vacation days like so many children of our generation: locked outside. Those were the days when young people were seen and not heard, and although we were pretty sure Grammy loved us, she had no patience for small children's noise and fidgety antics. Luckily for us, her neighborhood in the village of Veazie was packed with adventures just waiting for us to claim.

I fondly remember rolling down her grassy hill with my arms tucked tightly into my chest, feeling itchy from the overgrown lawn and fresh blackfly bites. She had a wall of lilac bushes behind her home with heart-shaped leaves and a dizzyingly sweet fragrance. Even as an adult, that smell instantly transports me to her backyard. I recall shading myself under Grammy's clothesline that stretched from her front steps to a pulley strapped to an old elm on the far side of her property. Grampy Butcher sometimes treated us to Cracker Jacks when we accompanied him on his beer and tobacco runs to Lancaster's Market. I can still taste the salty sweat of my forearm where I licked it to apply the temporary tattoo prize from the box of sweet popcorn and peanuts.

I regarded the Penobscot River with suspicion from her yard on the hill because she taught us to fear the potential danger if we got too close without proper adult supervision. It was necessary to teach us a fearful respect for the power of rushing water for our protection and our safety.

Across the narrow road from Grammy's house was a natural playground we referred to as The Ledges. It included a babbling rocky brook that was guarded by an old crabapple tree heavy with tiny sour fruit that had worm holes and inevitably gave us the trots. We snuck into the mysterious forest hoping to spot Bigfoot or a sidehill gouger. Orange pine needles carpeted the shady paths and hushed our footsteps while we searched for wildlife or a rare arrowhead arti-fact. Stephen and I found rabbits, frogs, birds, and spiders, but we never found any harm. These were safe woods for us. The only trouble we ever found was a hangout for teens who left empties and graffiti to mark their territory and assert their fledgling autonomy. It was a wild contrast against the gentle natural envi-ronment, but one that was unfortunately common in those days.

At the time, we only had one car that ran, so my parents coordinated rides and shared the vehicle. It was the same behemoth that so many families drove back then: a chocolate-brown full-sized Dodge van with a console that was per-petually sticky, either from spilled soda bottles or toppled beer cans, since there was no such thing as a cup holder in 1978, or a DUI. I remember my father swearing never to buy a Chrysler again as he cranked the ignition key repeat-edly and pumped on the gas pedal, trying to bring the beast to life. We loved it when Dad removed the backseats to transport his dirt bikes. That meant we could surf the big hills in the cluttered, greasy, corrugated steel playground with no side windows that smelled of two-stroke motor oil. Stephen and I belted the "Wipeout" song as we stood in the back of the van, braving the treacherous terrain of Bangor's Newberry Street. We spread our feet wide, bent our knees, and held our little arms out for balance and protection, since there were no seatbelts to keep us safe. We had the essential surfing skills that would help us become successful adults one day.

On one particularly hazy, hot, and humid summer afternoon, my mother rode her ten-speed bicycle up Route 2 along the river to Veazie. She was coming to pick us up after a long shift at the hospital. It was normal for Mum to pick us up after work, but all the previous times she brought the van. On this day, my dad needed the van. Parents didn't discuss their decision-making processes with their kids in the 1970s, so I have no idea why the van wasn't available on this day. Mum was cheerful when she arrived at her mother-in-law's house and explained to her young children that we were going on an adventure. We were going to walk the four miles home. To Elm Street. In Bangor. At the peak of summer temperatures. At that age, we had no concept of distance, so we struck out on our journey with high hopes and empty hands. Our mother led us home while she pushed her bike along beside her. We had no water. We had no sunscreen. We had no idea what kind of summertime nightmare awaited us for the next few hours of travel on foot.

The miles added up as we hobbled our way to Bangor. We caught glimpses of the rushing river and marked our progress with landmarks like Veazie's wooden bridge, Mount Hope Cemetery, and the Riverview Motel-No Tell. We found encouragement in the consistent driving flow of the river that rushed toward home and showed us the way to comfort and safety. We paused many times to rest in the shade. Mum apologized to us over and over for making us walk so far. We cried in our suffering, all three of us; the muddy tracks on our cheeks drew lines from our eyes to our shirt collars. Cars rushed by on their bustling way to get groceries or whatever distraction kept them from noticing a frustrated mother and her two sweaty babies.

We came upon Cascade Park late in the afternoon. Mum assessed her young family's emotional, mental, and medical needs and gave us the most amazing news I had ever heard in my few years on the planet. She told us to wade in the fountain! I protested that I didn't have my swimming suit. She insisted that we cool off in the tiny pool, which was painted light blue and constructed of concrete. It took some convincing to get me to break the rules and enter the water fully clothed, but once my toes touched that refreshing liquid, I abandoned all propriety. I ventured into Cascade's fountain, sharing my shallow swim with the floating bugs, and trying not to disturb the discarded litter and wishing coins resting on the bottom. I never in my wildest dreams thought I would have the full endorsement from my mother to take a dip in a public fountain. People stared. She didn't care.

We were going to be okay. Home was not much farther. We had endured the pain of heat exhaustion, blisters, sunburn, muscle cramping, thirst, and fatigue. The remainder of our journey was spent in higher spirits and lower core temps. Relief was in sight. We would sleep well that night.

That miserable day turned into a magical dream come true. The Penobscot led us home to security and comfort. Bruce Lee is famously quoted as saying "[water] can flow or it can crash." It can have the grace of a gentle trickle or the mighty force of destruction. The influence water has is all in the perception and application. The hazardous conditions that Grammy Butcher warned me about in my youth were equally as true and valuable as the guidance and comfort my mother taught me to draw from it on that hot day in the sun.

The river knew the way all along. The Penobscot would always show me the way home.

Empty Lot

MEG WESTON

I walk my dogs down Greenfield Street
named for fallow fields just waiting
for houses to spring from the earth.
With crack and thunder giant pines fall,

their branches stripped to feed the flames
logs stack up like bodies beside turned earth.
I see trees in conflagration, flames leaping into fog
of muddy spring in Maine. Fire clearing land,
snap crackle and pop of branches brings to mind

a childhood memory—foggy, tainted,
a smokescreen in the woods beyond
my bedroom window. Nightmares,
waking up to emptiness, my father taken
in an ambulance, sirens wailing.

I used to watch light filter through pines
on this corner lot in late afternoon, the sun
a prism refracting rays across stonewalls
marking boundaries of the empty lot.

That filtered sunlight through trees,
called *komorebi*—untranslatable
Japanese word for scattered light—
a word I didn't know I needed
until I lost those trees.

Brackish

Josh Kauppila

Flowing downstream, meeting the meanest at the delta
saltiest of wishes let the sand know what he felt, a
minute of your time but a half a days the tides blink.
In the open ocean breaks the hope and hopeless, all foam and motion,
is it truth or just what the mind thinks, at the edge where persistence
meets devotion if I can mind brinks.
Precipices precarious peaks,
valleys form mile-wide hints.
Horizon doesn't seem wide enough for these open heart stints,
the rocks roll back a bubbling half inch
the seaward wave
meets the landward wave
and neither flinch.

The Same Stream Twice

VALERIE CAMPBELL

Artemis arrived at the house on Tannery Stream with a dog, a 2006 Jeep, a broken heart, a fractured mind, and a shattered spirit. What little was left of that spirit seemed to be contained in the dog, who had slept through much of the twenty-five-hour drive up the coast.

She had returned home to Maine to fix an old and broken house on a few acres. For her, the selling point had been the long rambling stream that flowed down the property as gravity pulled it rushing into the Penobscot River, then a short way to the bay where it merged into the Atlantic Ocean.

The morning felt heavy, though the sun still lit the blue cloudless sky as it usually did. Gray thunder and rain would feel the same to her, and if the angel of death had appeared and said *Come along, it's your time*, she would have replied *Okay* and followed listlessly, as long as no effort was required. And though the logical part of her brain might have argued that grief was transient and depression part of that transition, emotion's voice seemed louder.

She unconsciously ran her fingers through her hair, touching the long scar that ran from the corner of her eye past the missing part of her ear. There was no one here to see, she thought, and that was good. It had taken her too long to get here. In the months following the shooting, she'd found herself on edge, jumpy, impatient to get through the endless tasks she set in her own way. Then yesterday, she'd simply stopped, abandoned the life she'd built, and fled back north.

She had driven twenty-five hours straight up the coast, her white-knuckled hands on the steering wheel, her service dog, Phoenix, buckled in beside her. Taking the bridge over Tannery Stream, she took a sharp right and turned right again down the dirt path that implied a driveway.

Artemis braked the old Jeep to a stop and sat for a moment gazing at the house, her hand still gripping the steering wheel. From inside the Jeep, the old Cape looked depressed, gray with black shutters, clinging to the downward slope of a long treeless hill. By the front door, a worn red chair sat among the weeds and beer cans glittered in the overgrown grass.

She wiped her palms down her jeans, forcing her breathing to slow before popping the Jeep's door open.

Nothing's wrong, she told herself. *I want this; I need this. Just keep moving.*

The German shepherd she'd named Phoenix jumped from seat to ground in a smooth muscled motion and she attached his short leash. But instead of entering the house immediately, they walked down the hill to the stream, something she had wanted to do since first viewing it.

Below them, the stream curved and twisted around rocks, water taking the least resistant path through weeds and apple trees as it spun past. Gone and still there. *Like memories*, Artemis thought.

She remembered that the stream should have a sound, one that she would never hear now. And birds. There should be the sound of birds.

She would never hear them again either.

But she could remember the sounds a stream made, almost hear it rolling and tumbling over the rocks, a whooshing sound that combined a low rumble with a sound like static. The sound vibrated in the earth, the scent, the movement, hypnotic. It almost created music, embellished by sounds remembered, floating softly through her mind.

She rubbed the tip of Phoenix's ear, feeling the soft fur, her thoughts slipping back, striking against a frozen moment in time. Her office. The black gun muzzle, the sound of it echoing, crashing against her head. The last sound she would hear.

It still resounded in her mind, all this time later. The scent of metal and the far-away unfocused look. Lying on the floor, she'd thought he was still breathing, fingers reaching, pushing into skin to catch his pulse. But then it was as if her mind had fractured. On one level she knew he was gone, dead. But that wasn't possible.

Time shattered—he was dead. He couldn't be dead. *He was dead—reverse time, let me go back. If there's a god, if there's magic, stay with me, stay with me—*

But that couldn't happen. It would never happen. She knew death had won again and the only way to fight it was to break her own mind. She'd stayed beside him, her own blood slipping into her eyes, holding his body next to hers, her face to his.

As her stalker ran away, others had run in, shocked, stunned. And later, worried that she wouldn't hold up against this latest onslaught of trauma and grief.

They shouldn't have worried, she thought. Between the frequent shocks of panic and cloying depression, she felt nothing now, her emotions numb. Always all or nothing.

She refocused, rubbed her face, her eyes, as if to remove the memories, forcing those thoughts away and breathed in the moist morning air. At the edge of the stream, she found sharp rocks chiseled into a shape resembling an imperfect rectangle. Old stream rocks were round, she remembered, worn from time and the elements.

These probably were for the house's fieldstone cellar, she thought, and for a moment allowed herself to marvel at the time and energy it would take to build a cellar this way. First digging the hole deep and wide, as wide as the house and deep enough to stand in, then splitting the rocks from the stream and carrying each one uphill to place, rock by rock, to build four walls.

How long had it taken? Weeks, months? A season? Valuable time with the winter at your back.

She followed this line of thought to the stream. Round rocks, crystallized magma, formed 420 million years ago buffeted by the stream until their edges were gone and smooth and round. And over them, flat and angular chipped rocks, hewn by man for a specific purpose. Why were these chiseled stones left behind? Half covered by moss now, edges wearing in the stream, though 200 years is nothing to a rock. Nothing to a stream.

Tossing her phone on the bank, she pushed off her shoes, tucked her socks inside them, and stepped into the water. Cool, caressing, it flowed around her as pebbles scraped and cut her feet. She curled her toes, creating an arch over them. Stepping from stone to stone, she sloshed to the large boulder on the other side of the stream, the one with a chisel pounded deep into its surface.

The metal spike stood up like a giant among the tiny ecosystem of moss and plants. She could almost see someone 200 years ago saying, "Ah, that's enough stone then," and with one last powerful hit, knocking the spike into the rock. "There, now. We're done with this."

She sat beside the boulder, examining the little ecosystem more closely. How like a little forest it looked. Like a home for small magical beings. But it wasn't, was it? There was no magic, no little creatures to discover, to prove myth and legend and even god.

The little moment of marvel slipped away. How could she feel aware and yet dull at the same time? As if she could get up and function, but there was no emotion to it, no personality left to feel the joy she logically knew existed but didn't have the energy to find.

For what? What was the point if everything just ends? What was the point of trying?

She knew the answer. *So stop asking what and why.*

The answer was zero. Nothing. A number, signifying nothing. Full of sound and fury and signifying absolutely nothing.

Perhaps I can understand the shooter, the stalker, more now, she thought. If life means nothing, then it means nothing to take it, or to take your own. And if you were angry enough, take those you blame with you, like a toddler throwing a temper tantrum, flailing out, self-absorbed, but wielding a gun and 180 pounds of muscle.

But she didn't want to be kind to the shooter, to give him excuses. For a moment, she scratched at the surface of numbness, releasing a little blast of the anger that seethed underneath. It surged up into rage like a whip lashing out, destructive and uncontrollable.

Like him.

It made her sick. Being numb gave her control.

Artemis slid down to the stream's edge and thought about death. She picked up one of the discarded flints, turning it over, exposing the underside of her arm, running rich with blue veins like streams running through dirt, rock, the earth.

Old rocks were round, but the discarded flints chiseled by man were sharp enough. She ran it softly down the length of her forearm.

The leash pulled against her wrist as Phoenix jumped, jerking the flint from her hand as he bit at the stream rushing by him. He tripped, falling face-first into the water, rolling once with the fast-moving current, yanking her toward him.

She rushed to pull him up, struggling, calming the excited city-dog who didn't totally understand what a stream was yet. She held him for a moment, feeling the wet cold through her shirt, then unhooked Phoenix's leash to let him run. Unbalanced on the slippery moss, she slipped, falling with a soundless splash into the stream.

The cold and wet shocked her and she tried to scramble up, slipping again, then just sat there in the cool water, letting it wash over her. It rushed against her skin without a sound, chilling and soft like the hollow howl of a wolf. Almost beautiful. Like a dream, smooth and gentle, speaking, saying something calm and strong. Artemis could stay here, stop fighting, just stay here and listen.

But with the cold came the numbness of skin, so different from the numbness of the mind. It froze her skin and woke her mind. It made her want to stand up and dry off and run to get warm.

Phoenix scrabbled over from the bank to yap at the stream. He bit at it and dodged back, bounced, and charged again.

Better to be like Phoenix, she thought, *than to be human*. Better to not ask questions without answers. Better to splash in the stream and fall in face-first and get back up and explore.

What was the saying—no one steps in the same stream twice for it is not the same stream and you're not the same person—or was it a river? The same river twice? She couldn't remember. It didn't matter. Watching the water swirl and rush past, dislodging the flint from the bank, dipping it under, she understood that. The flint drifted on the current like a bird on the wind and lodged on a crystal rock, perfectly round.

Artemis stood, dripping wet, and slogged her way to the bank, calling to Phoenix, now sitting in the stream, water ruffling his fur. She stood there a moment to watch the stream, now changed ever so slightly, because they walked through it, played, and fell down in it. And got back up again.

Her phone vibrated on the bank and she leaned down to swipe it up, wondering what now.

Where did you go? the text read. *I'm at the house. Where are you?*

She shivered, wet fingers on the screen, dropping the phone on the bank, picked it up, and tried to block the number.

You want me to find you. I always find you.

She hit the block icon, swiped at the screen, and turned it off, stuffing the phone down deep in her pocket.

"Not this time," she said, and ran with Phoenix back up to the warmth of the house.

Polar Vortex

HANS KRICHELS

Brrr ... Bitterly cold out there this morning,
smoke rising off the Penobscot,
caught up on the fringes, as we are, of this Polar Vortex
which is supposed to be swirling high in the stratosphere over the North Pole,
but somehow got split in half due to warm air rising
from a glacier that melted last summer
due to a blanket of greenhouse gasses
rising from smokestacks far to the south of here.

So the Polar Vortex got split in half, wobbled on its axis, spun out of control,
and settled over Chicago,
where chill factors plummeted, the Great Lakes froze,
frostbite and hypothermia ran rampant, eight people died from the cold,
and, here in Maine, we shivered on the shores of the Penobscot.

While the president of our Great Country spoke scornfully about
Global Warming,
how it was Fake News.

And a fourth grader in Tallahassee wrote an essay
begging her president to come back to school and learn what any kid knew,
about the warming of the oceans and the fouling of the air.
All the kids knew about that, about their planet in crisis.
And they struggled to respect, to even comprehend,
any adult, even a president, who told them it wasn't happening,
like some bogey-man in the closet
who wasn't really there.

Wild Song

LESLIE MOORE

The first loon calls from Penobscot Bay
after the dark season of silence.

His thin wail rises from the water,
bisects the rocky shore, traverses the street,

crescendos at my house. *Where are yooooou?*
he asks. *Where are yooooou?*

He has molted out of gray winter garb,
shimmied into prenuptial finery—elegant

in black and white, eyes gleaming red
in the gloaming. He throws back

his head, opens his throat,
releases his longing—

urgent.
I'm here! I answer. *I'm here!*

Vita Nuova

DOUG BARRETT

That first week in Maine, early June passing for October
I walked out of the tree-darkened path above the old dam site
      to look over the misty river.

At that moment she too stepped out of forest shadow
and waded the ankle-high channel to the little island
      where sandpipers go.

Her coat, to my western eyes, shone fiery red
not the familiar Nevada buff—
      not subtle enough.

She walked slowly onto the island and stood still as if she'd caught
wind of something. Was she aware of me?
      Probably not.

Then she stepped into the main channel, just below
the rapids, and soon was up to her neck in the Penobscot
      swimming across the strong flow

then hauling out on the far shore with a shake
and disappearing into the tree façade, I following behind
        in my mind.

Where was she leading me
mystic doe with her indifferent inscrutable summons?
        Nowhere, maybe.

Or maybe to a place of deprivation, grave
and obscure to all who'd scout it out:
crow's call, hawk's cry, brave

new world emptied of tangled love, commercial lusts—
homeless homes under drooping boughs, where like silenced gunshots
        acorns fall in today's gusts

dark world from which only eternal vigilance can arise
trance from which the haunted or hunted may never
        return to reveal paradise.

Thus Spoke the River

Emma G. Rose

My brother Shane and I sat on a pair of rocks just off the shore of the Penobscot River. If both of us reached out at the same time, we should have just been able to bump fists. Moonlight shimmered on the water all around us.

We knew we weren't really supposed to be in the park after sunset. You never knew who might be lurking. But the moon was full and bright, and we would have seen anyone coming a mile away.

We kept our voices low, because sound carried on the water. Shane was nagging me about my latest writing project, which had stalled somewhere between the inn and the dragon.

"You gotta put the words on the page, girl. That's where the magic happens." He gestured at me with his mostly empty Sprite bottle.

I rolled my eyes. "Thanks, Shia LeBeouf. You should make a YouTube series."

I flicked water at him. He retaliated by flinging the Sprite bottle at me. I swiped it away from my face and heard the plonk as it hit the water.

That's when things got weird.

The bottle shot back up and hit Shane between the eyes. I started to laugh. I couldn't help it. He looked ridiculous with water dripping down his face and the expression of a startled pug. The bottle splashed down again.

The water around us bubbled, and at the same time I thought I heard a voice. I couldn't make out words, just the sound. I looked at Shane to see if he had heard it, too, but he was staring at the bottle. It was floating much too high on the water and standing completely upright, even though I knew the water wasn't shallow enough for it to touch the ground. Somehow it stayed in that position, about a foot away from Shane.

"Is yours," the voice said. It was muffled, like the sound of your brother shouting at you from the dock when your head is underwater.

I jumped up, my bare feet gripping the rock, sure someone was in the park with us. Suddenly, I noticed every shadow cast by trees and boulders in the moonlight.

Shane stood up more slowly. It took me a minute to realize he wasn't looking around wildly, like I was. He was staring down at the bottle, which was rising up to meet him. Or maybe I should say the water was rising up to meet him. It wasn't a wave, but a column or maybe an arm, with the bottle on its open hand. I couldn't see fingers, but that's what it reminded me of. Like a waiter presenting your beverage on a tray.

"Take back," the voice said. It was clearer this time but still sounded like someone trying to talk underwater.

I shifted my feet, half-expecting an arm to reach out of the shallows and grab my ankle. For a long moment, nothing happened. The moon shone, the water flowed, Shane and I stood on our individual rock islands.

When Shane didn't move, the column rose a little higher, putting the bottle at chest height. "Yours," the voice said.

I could see the whites of Shane's eyes, the flash of his teeth, bared in a stiff grimace as he reached out and touched the bottle with his index finger. Nothing grabbed him. If anything, the world went a little more still, like even the river was pausing to see what happened next.

Shane pinched the neck of the bottle between his thumb and index finger and drew it toward him. The column of water fell away and disappeared.

A voice said, "Thanks you."

"Who are you?" The question I really wanted to ask was "what are you?" but that seemed rude.

"We are Penobscot."

"You're a member of the tribe? What's your name?" I wanted them to talk more, so I could tell where the voice was coming from.

"Are Penobscot."

"Yes, but what are you called?"

I didn't get an answer. Just a bubbling sound, like a fish sighing.

"Um." Shane was pointing at a lump in the river. A lump that was rising. My mind scrambled for an explanation. A person in scuba gear maybe, or a submersible drone with a loudspeaker? I know that sounds dumb, but either of those would have been a lot more reasonable than what actually happened.

The water didn't flow off the person as they stood, because the person was made of water. And it wasn't really a person, exactly. It had the vague shape of a head and shoulders, but no arms or legs. It didn't have eyes or a mouth or even any indication of where those things would be.

If you picture someone using a bedsheet as a Halloween costume, but the bedsheet is made of water and so is the person under it, you might get some idea of what I saw.

Shane patted frantically at his pockets. I knew he wanted to take a picture, but I also knew he'd left his phone in the car. I lifted my own phone and fumbled for the camera app.

"I am Penobscot," said the voice from the column of water.

"You are..." I paused, not quite believing what I was about to say, "...the river?"

"Yes. Please not to throw bottles in us."

"Why do you speak English?" Shane asked.

Good question.

"We learn. Humans always talk, talk, talk. Not learn to speak river. No attention."

"Well, you've got our attention now," Shane said.

"Good. We tell you. You tell them."

"Tell them what?" I was looking at the photo I'd taken. The moonlight flattened everything, making it almost impossible to tell there was a column of water standing above the river unless you knew what you were looking for.

"Tell people. No more bottles. No more sick. No more dirty. Tell them no more or else."

"Or else what?" Shane asked.

"Or else no more humans."

I hoped it was talking about natural consequences here, not threatening a Biblical flood or some kind of sentient tsunami, but with the language barrier and complete lack of expression, it was hard to tell.

"Why would they listen to us?"

"You humans. You tell. You tell all."

"Do you have any idea how many humans there are?" I asked.

The river harrumphed, and muttered something that sounded like "too many."

"We could make a video," Shane said, "of the river guy."

"With your phone boxes, yes." The pillar rose up higher, apparently excited about this idea. "That is how humans talk. You watch and we tell them ourself."

I felt bad, because the river seemed so enthusiastic about the idea, but I said it anyway. "No one would believe us." I was experiencing it and I hardly believed it.

The pillar of Penobscot swelled and receded very quickly. It looked exasperated. But maybe I was overanalyzing. I do that when I'm freaked out.

"They won't believe hearing? They won't believe seeing?"

"She's right. They'll think it's CGI or something."

"What cee gee aye?"

"Fake. They'll think it's fake."

"Humans," it said, and there was a weight of disdain in the word.

"I could..." I stopped. It was a stupid idea, but it was better than nothing. "I could write a story about it."

"How is that better?" Shane asked. "Stories aren't real either."

"That doesn't matter," I countered, "as long as they're true."

"Huh?"

I talked right over him, looking at the river.

"Humans are good at stories. It's how we share ideas. It's the ... the current that carries our thinking to new places."

Shane snorted a laugh. "You really are a writer. Should I fetch a typewriter and some scotch?"

I glared at him and he cackled to himself, knowing he'd gotten to me. It didn't matter. I was already imagining the story I could tell about the voice of the river on a full moon night.

"I'll tell them a story and it will make them think, and maybe they'll think twice about the river and what goes into it. But we'll need a real conflict, something to really hook them."

"Conflict? We tell conflict," the pillar said. "Twelve type of fish swim up from ocean back to hatching place to spawn. Now are heavy with mercury, not eggs. Dams in their way. Damn humans fill with trash and worse. Fish fight for lives. Fight for fry. Birds eat fish. They die too. Not enough fish, too much sick."

The pillar rose as it spoke, drawing up more and more of the water, pulling it back from the banks, like a preview of the drought to come.

"Too much sick. Everyone sick. Big people and small people. First people and new people. Human people and fish people and bird people. Bear and deer and skunk and squirrel people. All need us to survive. Need river. Need rain. Need tears to cry over what lost."

The pillar shrunk suddenly like a slumping man, water rushing back to fill the banks. Its voice fell to a low churn. "We are people. People must save us."

Shane spoke into the silence, "Damn. I wish I had recorded that."

"I'll write it all down," I said. I'd been taking notes on my phone, typing with both thumbs as it talked. "I'll write it all down and I'll tell them."

"Tell them," it said. "No time left."

"I will," I said. "I promise."

Whatever was holding it together let go and its form splashed down, dissolving back to the current. Instantly it was gone and there was nothing but the river.

I wondered how long that would last.

Watershed Haibun

KATHLEEN ELLIS

Katahdin is blurry because of airplane breath on the
window. Miles fly back and forth as I look for landmarks.
Soon we will be the bend in the river. I echo the trembling
of the plane, look down where the East and West Branches
converge. It's not that I cannot choose between them, but
I'm in a plane after all

> (which is why
> I begin to love air
> above water)

I Wish I Could Describe Winter Sky in Maine

JEAN ANNE FELDEISEN

Long, low clouds ironed out flat
a calm day forbids
       the action verbs
of snow or ice or wind

Is there a color that needs naming?
Gray?
     White?
              Nothing at all?

As clouds disperse beaded water droplets
     lag   suspended
        pearls of cloudiness

     The viscosity hinders sight
my fingers slip through emptiness

Sadness
     creeps
            like ground fog
The sun   darts out
     a half-hearted attempt
to soar above its feeble arc

Then it is dark

The River School

GEOFF WINGARD

I was a creature of the coast. I grew up in a small Maine fishing town filling bait bags for lobstermen, rigging yachts for the well-heeled summer residents of the midcoast. My grandfather had been a merchant seaman and longshoreman. I'd inherited his fid and marlinespike and made extra money in high school splicing fancy dock lines for tourists. And while I knew there were rivers that ran to the sea, I dismissed their subtle powers, distracted by my youth and by the raw urgency of the Atlantic.

I was nearly thirty years old when time and circumstances forced me upstream. I grudgingly made my way from the coast up nearly thirty miles of winding river to graduate school. Immersed in my work, I barely paid attention to the river that ran below my classrooms. That first year, I missed the sea desperately and longed for the sound of crashing waves on cobbles, the smell of salt on the wind, and the regularity and comfort of the tides. Surely I recognized the startling autumn colors reflected in still pools on the river. I shivered past the groaning of the winter's ice. I must have stopped on a bridge to watch dark spring water flood past, but I was a visitor, a mere tourist, and hadn't yet gotten to know the river.

I think it was fatherhood that began to change me. As my daughter began to crawl and then walk and then explore her world, I began exploring my own. We played together on the banks of the Stillwater River, the artificial oxbow of the Penobscot created, maybe, to depose the Native people of their land, throwing sticks in the spring flood and fishing for pumpkinseed sunfish from sunny summer banks. In those years, I was desperate for adventure, so in moments I could steal between classes, research, parenthood, and work, I'd find hidden spots along the banks of the big river, the Penobscot itself, where I'd sit just to listen to the rush of the water, imagining it would carry me somewhere else.

One day in early spring, in gray cold March, as I drove to the end of the road where I'd park my truck and walk down to the riverbank, I was startled by a voice of the Penobscot I hadn't heard before. A grinding, banging, violent voice. It matched my mood, and I quickened my pace, almost jogging to the riverbank as if I were afraid to miss something. I was greeted by a river in spring flood, whose power rivaled, in its own way, that of the ocean in winter storm. This river was no mere shadow of an ocean current—it was raw power, literally throwing the granite bones of Maine ahead of it as it coursed its way to the sea. For the first time I had the sense that the Gulf of Maine, which I had imagined drove the life of our communities, was, in reality, merely a gift of the great rivers—and the Penobscot River was the greatest of them all.

I stood awestruck watching, listening, and feeling the rumbling of the river in my chest. I ignored my cold feet. My coffee stopped steaming. I skipped my class. And in that moment I began to see the Penobscot for the first time as a visceral, powerful creature alive with the animating force of the world. It was my first day of river school as I began to look closely at the Penobscot and understand how the river shaped the lives and the very lands of those around it. It was my first day attending profound new lessons.

It's been two decades since that day when I stood on the banks of the Penobscot, but I haven't graduated from river school yet. I'm still taking lessons from the river. I'm learning how the seasons sound and smell differently along the riverbanks. I'm learning how dams chained the river's power and how their removal has given new life to the fish and birds and people of the riverlands. I'm learning how the history of humans' interactions with the Penobscot are written in the place names that surround it.

Once, I thought I knew a secret of the sea. I thought that the anonymity of its landscape gave it universal power, but now I'm learning something different. I'm learning that the intimacy of the river, winding in and out of people's lives, changing with the seasons, giving life to communities and cultures, may be a more human, and no less powerful, force in the world.

Spring Running

KARA DOUGLAS

Silver and wakeful the darting begins
near the foaming underbelly of the falls.
The alewives aim upstream,
tails flapping in rapid succession,
bodies scaling the steps of the stone weir,
muscling through the current.
There are so many,
my daughters reach into the water
and catch them by hand.

In the streambank shadows,
two sharp eyes that don't stop watching,
two rows of needle-like teeth and a furred body,
flexed and honed.
In one quick snap, the fisher engulfs the fish,
devours body and bone, the marrow of being,
then vanishes into the forest.

One life form becomes another,
passing the flame between them,
each an expression of something vaster than themselves.
Roots reach deep as the soil is renewed,
as this place persists, great heart pulsing.

She Is the Waves

Mo Drammeh

I watch the river, and she runs through the waste.

The Penobscot is my life. What little food I scrounge, I find by her banks. She is the water I drink. It is not fit for consumption; she was never meant to be consumed. She never could be.

She laps and she wails. She is not strong anymore. I know it. Her waters were once a mighty blue but have since been muddied by the dying of the light. The waves are nearly black. She has been poisoned. The wealth of minerals and riches she once held, taken away, dissolved into nothing. I know she must think of them. How little she cherished them when she had them. How much she needed them. The memories that were joyous to her only deepen the wound. I see her in my mind, her youth. Her strength, moving silently, streaming tears down Maine's rocky face. That face has been burnt away; all that is now is ash and water.

When I taste her waters, there is the grit: the unkindled cinder sliding across my tongue, brittle remains of the world that was. I do not blame her for this. She must carry us, what we had. She moves, and we move with her, guided in death, shepherded into the after. Around her, there is the barren: gray and black, gray and black, the sky almost permanently stained with black, as if a storm approaches, too lethargic to ever arrive, stuck in the liminal space of dread. I am thankful for it. It blocks out the sun, the world-killer, incensed at life in all its forms, burning all it could land its gaze upon.

I do not know how she fares out from under the smoke. I do not care to know. I see the edges of those poison clouds, where the burning sun above peers over, and the land is cast alight once again. But I see her here, and here she runs.

She runs toward, and she runs away, but by all means she will run. She will not stop. Her flow is an anomaly. All here has been brought to a still—no commerce, no thought, no progression. Not her. She is defiant, forever defiant. She lives when we cannot, rolling across the edge of oblivion with all the strength she has left, a wave of pure will, sickly and broken, but moving. She holds us, or what remains. Determined to take us forward.

I find myself at her shores, broken, only knowing her strength. I know I will return to her one day. Soon. I know it. And when it comes, she will let me fall into her, arms open, and we will become one, two wills combined. She will return to what she was. She is too stubborn, too occupied, running headlong into the future, to be stopped. And I shall be beside her, a ripple in those crashing waves, ebbing and flowing for time immemorial.

The Blood Moon Tolls

MEG WESTON

On the day of the blood moon eclipse,
we awakened to a morning hymn of waves

pounding rocks outside the rented cabin.
We visited a bell foundry that day,

watched flames liquifying bronze bars
poured into molds cast of sand,

transfiguring essence into sound—
bronze bells and wind chimes.

At sunset, watched the full moon rise
over an expanse of yawning sea.

Before the eclipse,
        we held hands.

Before the darkness came,
moonlight shimmered on the waves.

Before the death-knell;
Before the call that came around eight;

Before the words: Overdose. Heroin. Fentanyl.
Before red blood congealed in blue-black veins.

Long before this occultation, a rising swell of opioids,
swept in its wake a hundred thousand lives that year.

We wept and lay awake all night staring at the ceiling
while the earth's shadow stole the moon, until

just a sliver remained illuminated by the sun. Red light
of a thousand sunsets cast upon its lunar surface.

Earth's orbit followed its course, eclipsed the moon
in penumbra. Earth's specter lengthening its red light umbra.

The longest eclipse of our century,
the longest shadow.

Restoration

PATRICIA SMITH RANZONI

In commemoration of June 11, 2012, Penobscot River, Maine

The dawn the dam removal begins
rises as an ancient salmon-pink current
rivering the East, given again.

A woman downriver, born
to its flood, wakes at four knowing
that eagle feathers are being lifted
to pray in a day of praisegiving.

While her mate dreams, she strikes her flame
and listens outside in bird and insect singing,
blossom and new leaf smell, as darknesses
give way to a new day in every sense.

Ancestral fish-urges to return
power her thrust *she must go.*

Without constraint, she slips in
and begins to swim home.

No dam can stop her.
She will hurl herself with the others
until she dies.

Tavern on the River

Morgan Campbell

It was a clear, quiet day at the Muddy Cuddie Tavern on the Maine coast until a group of four men entered. They chose a table, their gaze shifting to the old bridle hanging above the fireplace, its leather worn with age and the polished metal marred with a patina at the edges. Their hushed tone and searching eyes were noticeable to anyone who looked in their direction.

The bar maiden, bigger than the six-foot Scottish barkeep, approached, taking the men's orders on a sheet of paper as she tried to chat. Every attempt at talking ended when one of them took an awkward glance at the bartender, whose steely gaze would meet theirs.

The old Scot manning the bar heard a muttered phrase. "He really does have a bridle up there."

The barkeep huffed, amused at the new curious patrons, taking the paper handed to him by the bar maiden. "Yer' here about my tale, aren't ye'?" The barkeep prepared their drinks.

The men froze, each staring at the old Scot, jaws slacked and eyes dumbfounded. "Yes, sir, we are." One man's voice trailed off, embarrassed.

"A wool coat is an odd choice this time o' year." The bartender nodded at the men.

One man spoke up among the whispers, stuttering his words, avoiding eye contact. "It's a bit cold out today."

The barkeep snorted, letting his quiet laugh die down. "It's August." He set the drinks down for the bar maiden to take. Lifting the tray, she returned to the men's table. Sand dusted off her hair as she set the beers before them.

"Yes sir we, uh..." one man started to say. They whispered to each other as one elbowed another. "We're fishermen, sir, wanting local stories of the Penobscot River," a man with brown hair said, his gaze glancing at the bridle over the fireplace.

"Aye, I'm sure ye' are." The bartender glanced at his server, who smiled in response, setting the tray down. He took a breath and began his story.

"When I was a younger lad, I worked as a fisherman, much like yerselves. It was nearing dusk and the end o' my time fishing. The waters were mucked with runoff from the papermills. My catch was poor, but I thought nothing of it. After all, the mills were growing, and this town needed the work. I hated seeing the place where I grew up change. After the mills went up, all the fishin' and gross shite—." The old Scot trailed off. He took a breath, gathering his thoughts. "But that's not the story yer' here for. There I was, reeling in my line, ending my run for the evening, when I saw a sight I still can't believe."

"Was it a sea serpent?" one of the men asked.

The barkeep smiled at the thought. "Nae, it was a horse! A damn horse, with a bridle, saddle, an' all."

"A horse?" one of the men asked.

"Aye, a bonnie big Clydesdale wanderin' along the shore. Imagine the luck! The poor beast looked half-starved."

"We heard you saw a—" one man started to say, but the old Scot stopped him.

"Ye' probably did—folk like their stories. Now, I did what any poor lad would do and headed for the shore. A free horse and an expensive one at that. Easy pickings, I thought. Mind ye'. I was a bit daft at the time."

"A bit?" the server spoke. "Yer' still a bampot ye' are."

The barkeep mulled over the thought. "Aye, she ain't wrong."

"What does a horse have to do with that? Was there something wrong with it?" one of the men asked.

"Ye' best believe there was. Here I am, a Scottish lad raised on tales of home, and I didn't question seeing a damn kelpie!" The Scot maintained a jovial smile despite his raised voice.

The Scottish maiden laughed. "Ye' still don't, ye' silly fool." She turned to a man with a blue hat. "Are ye' finished with that?" She gestured to his empty mug.

The man handed it to her. "Yes, dear, thank you." He nodded, his skin flushed as he stared into the woman's eyes.

"Best not catch feelings fur that one. She's more than ye' can take."

The man in the blue hat tilted his head, looking the bar maiden up and down. One of his colleagues bumped him on the shoulder, and his face reddened.

"Now, I'm rowing my way tae the horse, keeping still tae not startle it. I watched the horse step intae the water and noticed something that saved my life. The beast looked wet and sandy. Like it had just come outae the water."

"How did that save you?" a man asked.

"Ye' should know why. Yer' hunting this beast, aren't ye'?"

One man audibly gasped as the jaws of the other three slackened. "No, sir, of course not. That would be preposterous!"

"Easy there, laddie, yer' not the first to look for the beast and yer' not the last."

"So there really are monsters in the Penobscot?" one man asked, standing. The bar maiden glared at them. The other two slugged their beers and stood to leave.

"Aye, but they're the least of ye' worries. The fish could barely survive those waters. Ye'd be damn lucky if those beasts are still around."

The men hesitated, whispering to each other, then returned to their seats.

"Since ye' don't know, I'll tell ye'. Be suspicious if ye' ever see a horse or lass near the water. The kelpie can change their shape. If that horse looks wet or has sand in her hair, best leave it be."

"What did you do?" a man with short, brown hair asked.

"What do ye' think I did? I turned that boat around and paddled my way tae the other shore, but she knew I was ontae her. I heard a splash behind me, and the horse was gone. She was in the water chasing me."

"How did you get away from it?"

"I've got nae a clue. I paddled that boat till my arms were sore, but it was faster. The beast headed me off, popping its head above water, nearly knockin' me off my boat, its eyes wide and mad. The beast was like a normal horse, but its skin looked pale and blue. Its teeth were sharp like a dog's. I could see the desperation in its eyes, green with slits like a cat's. I grabbed my box of fish, chucked it at the beast's head, and paddled away."

"Did it follow you?" the man in the blue hat asked.

"It tried to, but the fish that leaped from the box distracted it enough for me tae get away. I thought myself fortunate. Poor thing swam after those fish like its life depended on it." The old Scot glanced at the bar maiden. She smiled back.

The men paused until one spoke up. "You felt bad for it?" he asked.

"Aye, I did. Imagine living in that muck with nae a bite to eat. And it gets worse—one of the nets drifting in the water tangled around the poor bastard."

"Why is that bad?" the man with brown hair asked.

"Because I pitied the poor beast. We ruined its home, and it pays for it. So I did the most daft thing I could and went after it. Mind ye', I had to save the beast without touching it. I rowed right up next to it, grabbed my fish knife, and cut at the net. The kelpie rocked and kicked, knocking me outae my boat."

The bar maiden spoke. "Such an oddly fortunate situation inae."

"Why's that," the man with the blue hat asked.

The barkeep glanced at the server, giving her a quick grin. "You'll see."

"Did it come after you?" the man with brown hair asked.

"Nae, it was panicked. Didnae take long fur the beast to tire. It made my job easier until I touched it. Like the fables say, one touch and like sap, yer' hand sticks to it. Lucky for me the beast was already worn. Not only that but while working the net off, I grabbed the beast by its bridle. Grab a kelpie's bridle, an' it's yers'. I clear the net off the beast and go to land, expecting a fight, but nae, it goes along with me. We reach the shore, and it climbs out of the water, looking like a Clydesdale again. The beast released my hand, but it didnae attack me. It waited, watching me."

"That's ridiculous. Why would it let you command it?"

The old Scot laughed. "Have ye' been listening tae a word I've said? This whole speil is ridiculous! But if you think that's unbelievable, then you won't believe that it let me ride it." The Scot pointed to the horse's bridle hanging above the fireplace. "That's yer' proof right there."

Quietly whispering to themselves, the men soon turned back to the barkeep. "Please continue. What happened on the shore?"

"Nothing. We rested, then the kelpie let me hop on and ride it intae town. Odd looks we got. Both of us drookit. Ye' could see the trail o' water we made!"

"What happened to the kelpie?" the man with the blue hat asked.

"I kept her. She helped me with the fishing job until I worked up enough to afford this place. We found a better spot to fish. Ye' wouldn't believe how useful a water horse is. After that, I let her free."

"Freed? Why would you do that?" The man with the brown hair, hands on the table, nearly lept from his chair.

"Inae my place to keep a wild beast captive. They have their purpose."

"Did you ever see another?"

"I'd say I've seen the same one once or twice since then." The bar maiden shot him a look. The old Scot dismissed her with a wave of his hand. "But another?

I've never given it a chance. If ever I saw a horse on the shore, I didnae stick around to find out."

"The first one worked out for you, didn't it? Why not go for another?"

The Scot mulled his thoughts over, looking at the bar maiden. "Aye, but luck's not a thing tae push too far. Nor do I want to. Our river's havin' enough trouble comin' back as it is."

The men talked among themselves. A few words, debating what to do, reached the Scot's ears. Once finished, the brown-haired man spoke. "We appreciate you and your wife's time."

The barkeep laughed, big and hearty. "Oh lad, no, she's nae fur me."

The men exchanged glances, confused, looking at the bar maiden's hand for a ring that wasn't there.

"Odd a lady such as yourself is unmarried," the man in the blue hat said.

"Aye, only one man was strong enough to tame me. It didnae work out."

The men stood, pulling money from their wallets.

"Nae, don't worry about it. Promise to drop whatever daft plan ye' have, and ye' can keep yer' money."

Some of the men placed money on the table, but others didn't. They talked among themselves for a few minutes. The brown-haired man stopped the chatter. "We'll talk later," he hissed at the small group, then glanced at the Scot. "Thank you both again. It was a pleasure." They turned for the door.

"Aye, stay safe out there. And don't go bringing any kelpies back. They're more trouble than they're worth." He glanced at the bar maiden with a grin.

"Says the daft man who went after me," the bar maiden whispered, striking the old Scot with a soft thump of her tray.

The man with a blue hat turned around, staring at the Scottish maiden. "Wait. Are you..." he started asking but shook his head and walked out the door.

my boat drifts

LISA PANEPINTO

teeth-chiseled logs
guarding beaver
den hidden
in sand burrows

at home
in black waters
silt clouds
alive with
each movement

living off bark
ferns and cattail
eel grass
making water
clear for fish

tiger swallowtail
flying over
shimmering current

ever present
teaching us
to glow
with leaves

swim in silent
tree prayer

Hexagenia

MATT BERNIER

We wait all year for the *Hexagenia* hatch,
green mayflies rising out of Daicey Pond

so delicate and vulnerable that July's peace
never lasts, brook trout in regimental colors

charging and slashing in deep twilight
as we canoe across the polished stage,

no appreciation for our delivered lines
until we realize this theater isn't for us,

mere actors with our fly rods as props,
snagging the dark curtain of an evening,

dropping pieces of the set with a clatter;
it's not amateur hour, so we sit down,

shut up, flocked orchestra still chirping,
enjoying a ballet set during wartime.

Osprey

JAMES BRASFIELD

Open sky, high tide
and steady breeze, an osprey
circling out over the cove,

then kiting to hover

over fins' ripples, then plummets

feet first and light of day
passing through expectation,
the descending weight plunging

through the opaque surface
to instinct's depths, propulsion
to the bluegills, talons into one of what is there,

then uplift, the rising from the cove,

the fish, claw-held—sustenance
suspended head first and parallel
under the bird calling out,

wheeling back to arrival at twigs
and reeds thatched atop
the rusted smokestack

of a beached trawler, the nestlings there,
heads wobbling above
the thick crown,

the magnet when winter ends—

here, the tearing away
bits of fish
into open beaks.

Thin clouds float high over the nest.

I imagine something like smoke rings
forming in the nestlings'
tufted heads, and the impulse strong

for the pause and plunge.

Keep Heart

Josh Kauppila

keep heart with frogs, dear
rustling salmon where
the waters clear
fast shaded and pebble-y
trailing staccato owl call rings
through maple tops.
loon opens haunting organ stops
after coyote whines
with a glee that has sadness
and fear behind.
feel, if you may, woodpecker's knocks
as if the tree were your spine
or spring out, an inflated exploring
mushroom from underground mycelium veins
sleep like a sap-drawn tree
laying still in dream-roots as the
seasons change.
feel the feast of the rain—
and breathe out your gift
to the Sun.
keep heart with the frogs, dear
and the day has begun

A Letter from the Penobscot River Serpent as Dictated to Ryan George Collins

RYAN GEORGE COLLINS

Dear humans,

~~My name is~~ You would know me as the Penobscot River ~~Monster~~ Serpent. You may remember seeing a video of me a few years ago, though most of you probably wrote me off as nothing but a floating log. Well, I assure you that I am a very real creature, but I don't live in the river anymore. That video was of me swimming out to sea. I now reside in the Atlantic Ocean, but I'm writing this to let you know that I'm still watching you.

I'm sure you know that the Penobscot used to be a mess, filled with pollutants and dammed up with no regard for wildlife. It was in this filth that I was born. My parents were common American eels, mind you, but thanks to what you did to the water, I burst out of my egg ~~as a monster~~ different. I was already large for a newborn, and I grew unnaturally fast. I produced limbs which my fellows lacked, and I figured out how to use them by crawling along the riverbed. One night, I crawled onto the land just to see what was there, and it was only when I returned to the water and saw the shock of every creature around me that I realized my unique ability to breathe air. I also realized that I was far more intelligent than those I shared the river with.

This intelligence led me to figure out more about myself. As I swam up and down the river and explored its various tributaries, I quickly deduced how I had come to be. It had something to do with the toxins that flowed from the land into the water. While others shied away from the poison or withered at its touch, it invigorated me. Even today, the iridescence of an oil slick induces hunger when I see it. I reasoned, therefore, that these poisons were what made me different.

RIVERS OF INK: LITERARY REFLECTIONS ON THE PENOBSCOT | 57

I believe you call the process "mutation." Moreover, I was a healthy mutation, which also made me unique. Other mutations have been born in the river, but I am the only one who ever reached adulthood.

Upon learning what I am, I then began to wonder why I existed. Was I simply a random freak who was just lucky? Or had I survived and grown ~~into a monster~~ for a purpose? This was going to be harder to figure out, since, to my knowledge, I was the first creature in the river who had ever asked this question.

My resemblance to driftwood proved to be advantageous, as it allowed me to get close to your boats and shorelines to listen. It took me a while to understand what you were saying. I don't know how to measure time, but I do know that multiple winters passed before I had a firm grasp of the language. As I listened, I learned that the toxins were carelessly dumped into the water with no thought for what consequences might come. To be blunt, then, my birth was your fault. You had caused so much damage to the river that the birth of ~~a monster~~ something such as myself was inevitable.

What really stunned me, though, was even though you humans were aware of what you were doing, you kept on doing it. Despite still needing them to survive, I came to view the toxins that gave me strength differently as I connected the dots. Perhaps I was merely a lucky freak, and I was growing strong while the rest of the river died. I was anomalous, born despite the will of nature, something that was not meant to be … yet I was.

The personal turmoil this caused me steadily gave way to grim determination. If I had truly been born by chance without a purpose, then I would *make* a purpose for myself. My desire for purpose was driven by rage as I saw the river dying, so I directed that rage at you.

I moved slowly, I admit, for I wished to be methodical. I struck infrequently, a fisherman here, a kayaker there, people whose vanishing would be written off as just the risk humans take when entering the wild. That way, I figured, you would not suspect me until I was big and strong enough to strike at you with full force. Yes, that was what I determined I would be: the avenging spirit of the Penobscot River, ~~not a monster but~~ its sacred protector. I would nestle into the silty bottom of the river each night and dream of the day I would rise, the day I would make humanity regret what it had done. Gradually, I grew bolder, and disposed of a few individuals on whom the full burden of guilt lay. "Executives," I think you call them. They leave a terrible aftertaste.

Clearly, though, I waited too long for the day of reckoning to come. I'm not sure when I first noticed it, but it dawned on me one morning that the water felt different. I had always known it as a polluted, poisonous, murky place, but on that morning, the sensations I felt were ones I could not describe. The fish around me seemed to like it, though, so I determined that this change was not for the worse. It was only at the end of that day when I was finally able to describe these sensations. Clear was the word. The water was far less murky than it was before, and blues and greens shown in crystalline hues such as I had never seen before. As I continued to observe you over the months that followed, I heard you speak of how the water was cleaner, and how your efforts to prevent pollution and restore natural order to the river had been successful. I confess that I was tempted to attack some of the people I heard this news from, but I restrained myself, curious to see if this trend would continue.

The water has remained clean for many winters since I first heard that news, and after some deliberation, I decided that my presence is currently not needed. That video where you saw me for the first time was taken the day I swam out of the Penobscot River and into the Atlantic Ocean. I didn't mean to be spotted, but I suppose it was fortuitous that I was, because now you might take what I am about to say more seriously.

Everything I have learned about you humans tells me that you have a tendency to repeat behaviors, including those that are detrimental. You see, I'm not in the river anymore, but I remain nearby, paying attention to the fresh water that flows into the sea. It has remained clean thus far, and you have certainly done well in keeping it that way, but ... as a product of your previous actions, I don't entirely trust you. If I sense the water clouding again, I will return to the river, and on that day, you ~~had better run~~ will all know that I exist.

Please, do not give me a reason to return.

Regards,
The Penobscot River Serpent

A Tree

MICHELLE CHOINIERE

A tree stands tall with its friends,
A man cuts its feet,
It starts to bend.

Snap, the quickest monologue,
Friends all watch,
From tree to log.

A log pulled amongst its neighbors,
Pushed, rolled, and tumbled,
Man's fruit of labor.

Splash, the log begins to swim,
Through new places,
Along the river's rim.

Lonely drifting down the course,
The river guides it,
With strength and force.

Smack, ahead the sound is heard,
It grows and grows,
Curiosity stirred.

Logs gather by number unknown,
Together shuffling,
No longer alone.

The Forest, It Lay Bare Now

"Twinkle" Marie Manning

The forest, it lay bare now.
Trees no longer
Reach the sky;
The bird no place to land.
Trees no longer
Transform the air;
The bird no place to land.
Ask thou please,
Transform the air;
Impossible the plight.
Ask thou please,
Replant the trees;
Impossible the plight.
We need our roots;
Replant the trees.
The children cry,
We need our roots.
Reach the sky,
The children cry;
The forest, it lay bare now.

Turtle Eggs

Doug Barrett

What told me to come here today to the Salmon Club deck
and gaze over the river as it sparkles upon the rocks
and then told me, after half an hour watching the tree swallows
dart over the water, to get up and take a look down the steep grassy slope?

She'd dug deep, this snapping turtle, with clawed paddlefoot
a few yards downhill, tamping against the sides of the hole
the earth she couldn't lift out. To this height above the river she's trekked alone
to lay her eggs in the killing zone—the human zone, the skunk-fox-raccoon zone.

Now, in the sweltering June heat, she's resting between contractions.
At last she lifts a wrinkled baggy-panted leg
and from jacked-up abdomen
extrudes the wet white egg, almost as big as a ping pong ball

tamped by her hind foot deep into earth. Another and then another
each quickly squeezed out after long pause and mercilessly tamped down.
Here comes one more, the seventh. And before that how many? Twenty? Forty?
More? Her organs must pay a price to hide them all.

Who would have thought the old girl had so much life in her?
The paddlefoot rakes back the displaced dirt as she stares straight ahead, pig nose
goblin eyes, then turns slowly for the descent, dragging stegosaurian tail
down the path her ancestors must have labored up long before it was paved

maybe before humans ever saw this land, down over the concrete slab
through the ribbed rock, the dried bottomland mud
past the blood-red sumac stalks
through the bare willow snags and out onto the polished shore rocks

progress now accompanied by human procession
boys chattering praises to the awesome river queen
amazed at her flat gouged memory-scarred head
devoutly following turtle mother a little way into the river

perhaps someday themselves to be reborn,
by memory of her, from their electronic sacs.

Camp Hope

ELLIANA LABREE

I used to get all dressed up for these appointments and take a mini photo shoot before we went inside. Today, I just wasn't feeling up for it. Instead, I had decided to wear a hoodie and shorts and figured maybe I'd take a photo later, so I could reminisce.

I stepped out of the car.

"Do you want to get a photo in front of the building, Ellie?" my mother asked.

"I'm good," I replied.

We walked into the tall building, and the next thing I knew we were in the elevator. The ride up was quiet, which allowed my anxiety to grow. The elevator dinged, and we stepped off into the silent, lengthy hall. We walked down the hall toward the door that I knew led to the waiting room. The nauseating smell of the room immediately triggered memories of my time there.

We walked up to the front desk. I looked around the room, and as I saw the blue-painted slab of wood that said "Camp Hope," thoughts of camp came streaming back. It had been so fun, and I'd made many friends who struggled with the same feelings and problems I had. It was nice to be around people who got it.

"Hold out your arm."

I was brought out of my thoughts to see an expectant nurse waiting with a hospital bracelet. I stuck my arm out reluctantly as the nurse clipped the bracelet onto my arm. The thin plastic looped around my wrist sharply pressed against my skin. I wonder if they knew how much these bracelets victimized their patients. If only I'd been saving my hospital bands from the beginning. Countless now.

After a while sitting and waiting to be seen, a nurse finally called my name and ushered us into a room. I took off my sneakers and climbed under a wall measure so they could take my height and stepped onto a scale so they could take my weight. Next came the part I had been dreading.

The nurse took a needle the size of the Eiffel Tower off the tray. "Which arm do you prefer?"

Neither is what I wanted to say. "My right."

I looked away. I felt the nurse tie a tight rubber band around my arm and started feeling around for veins. She let go, got up, and walked to the other tools. Returning, she scrubbed my vein harshly with scratchy cotton. I clenched my fists, and my breathing quickened. I snapped my eyes closed and felt a sharp sting in my forearm.

It felt like an eternity, but the needle was gone, and I had acquired a new Dora the Explorer Band-Aid. We were ushered to an examination room. This one had a firm foam hospital bed and two plastic chairs. I hopped up on the bed onto crinkly paper I thought I might rip. "Do you want any snacks?" the nurse asked.

"Sure," I replied.

She left and returned with peanut butter crackers and ginger ale, staples of basic, unflavored hospital food. Then, she exited the room again and left me and my mom to wait for the blood test results.

I lived with this fear in the back of my mind. I'd try to ignore it, but sometimes it would catch up to me, especially in the hospital. All my normal thoughts were overridden by loud, pounding voices shrieking about how I was going to die one day, and—

I turned on my phone. Scrolling through Instagram was the best way to drown out my thoughts.

Then came the sound of the wood door squeaking open, and clunky footsteps startled me. I looked up. A familiar face. She was here. It was time.

"Hey, Ellie."

It was my oncologist. My cancer doctor.

"Hey," I replied.

She asked me a series of questions about my health, and I told her how I'd been doing. My head buzzed through it all, and the walls of the room drew in. Then she finished up her exam by telling us the test results.

"Well, there is no evidence of disease in your tests!"

I don't know what I was expecting, but it was probably that. It had been eight years already since I last had cancer, so why would it come back so late? And yet, I don't like thinking about the possibility of me having cancer again and not catching it in time and dying before high school is over. I had known too many people who had their cancer either kill them or survive it and then have it come back but worse.

Dying young is one of my biggest fears in life. I mean, obviously everyone will pass eventually, but I want to accomplish something first, past middle school. I want to be a social worker. I want to help kids who are young and have had rough childhoods, to be someone to support them and understand what they're going through. This is my dream job. I want to be someone who I needed when I was young.

"You guys are free to go!" she said.

I thanked her and headed out the door back to the front desk.

Death. Something little Ellie with cancer didn't understand. Something older Ellie now still doesn't really understand. What happens after death? Nobody knows. I think that's the scary thing. The unknown. Just like I'll never know why I was picked, at only five years old, to have a life-threatening disease.

As my mom and I strode out of the hospital, relieved, I also felt angry about how this is a never-ending cycle of hospital visits. Eventually, once they believe that my cancer has a low enough chance of coming back, they say they'll start spacing them out less frequently, until, hopefully, I stop going entirely.

Editor's note: Imagine a place where young heroes battling cancer and blood disorders trade hospital halls for hiking trails and medical charts for campfire songs. Welcome to Camp Hope—a transformative summer haven, a partnership between the Northern Light Eastern Maine Medical Center and the Bangor YMCA. Nestled on the idyllic northern shores of Branch Lake, one of the many lakes that make up the lower Penobscot watershed, this weeklong adventure offers more than just outdoor activities. It provides a sanctuary where kids can momentarily forget their health struggles and revel in the simple, unfiltered joy of being a kid.

Hot Cocoa

ALICE MAY HOTOPP

When my dad laughed, he bellowed. His round cheeks warmed with color and squeezed his eyes into slits; his mouth opened wide as if he were mid-shout. When he really got into it, he threw his head back or bent forward at the waist, his arms wrapped loosely over his stomach as if trying to keep his body from laughing itself to pieces.

*

Packing up camp after breakfast, Elliot, my partner of barely two months, found a Ziplock bag of cocoa powder under the picnic table. He held it out to my mom, who, in the middle of organizing the food while others loaded the canoes, stared at the bag in his hand. "That's Ken," she said simply. Elliot's eyes widened. He glanced quickly down at the bag, then back at my mom. "Those are Ken's ashes," she repeated. "I left them under the table so they wouldn't get mixed up with the food." She began to shake her head and giggle, the giggle breaking into a full laugh. Soon we were all rattling with laughter, knowing my dad would have found nothing funnier. Still laugh-sighing and wiping our eyes with shirtsleeves, we waded into the lake where it ran clear over a shallow sandbar. My mom opened the Ziplock. Passing the bag among his wife, daughters, and lifelong friends, we let my father's ashes drift into Lobster Lake. As I let the dust that was once my father's hands slide through mine, I began to shake again, my bones screaming with the sweetest, purest longing that a body can hold. My dad's ashes swirled with the current and dissipated, returning to the water to be absorbed by the roots of watershield, to drip off the muzzles of grazing moose, to be integrated into loon eggs, to fill our water bottles, to drift down the Penobscot to the sea. I folded into a crouch, gave my body over to my mother's and Elliot's hands on my shoulders, over to the waves of cool wind and water. I gave my body over to life that folds into and over itself again and again and again, that flows from one being into the next like rivulets of water, that ebbs from tears of mirth to grief and back, that fills our hearts and bellies like a steaming mug of cocoa, warming our hands before they turn to dust and return to the water.

The Woman Walked to the Mailbox

Kristen Clanton

The boy grumbled when she put her hand on the front door.

"Just watch through the window," she said. "Watch me walk the stairs and sidewalk. Follow the line of the river as it angles toward the road—get your stool and watch through the window."

The boy kicked his legs off the couch and stood in front of the television. Elmo was dancing on a black stage behind the boy's head. Furry red arms and legs came out of the boy's ears.

The boy turned to the window. A furry red arm came out of his mouth.

"I can't see the mailbox," the boy said.

The woman looked out the window. The snow was fat-bellied for March. It fell under the full force of gravity without wind, like millions of the boy's tiny army men, jumping from planes without parachutes. The woman frowned. Fog grasped at the rafters, the river. She couldn't see one rapid, one stone.

"I'll wear my red scarf— you'll see me."

The boy whined. "But you won't see me."

"Wear your red hat."

The boy sighed. The woman had finished knitting the red hat and red scarf just yesterday, the fibers still stiff with unuse.

"I'll be so fast," the woman reassured him.

The boy dragged his feet along the rug but went to the bathroom to get his stool.

The woman heard a scraping sound, boots on wood. It was heavier than she imagined.

"Aunt Caroline sent you an Easter package," the woman called down the hall. "Don't you want the chocolate bunny?"

The boy emerged from the dark, the stool bumping against his shins. He smiled when he put the stool by the window, smiled when he put on his red hat.

But it was a new smile—a harried one the woman didn't know. She put on her red scarf and opened the door. The boy grimaced. She didn't really want to go.

Outside, she heard the river rushing through serpentine turns, the sound of wet snow falling from the skeleton trees. She saw the boy through the window, rubbing his eyes. He knocked twice on the glass. The woman waved. Her hands were cold.

When she got to the bottom of the stairs, she saw the boy's red hat. She pretended she could see his dark hair, his big eyes. She thought she heard the telephone. As the woman walked along the river, she imagined the boy at the window. Once, she turned around and waved, the face of the fog at her back.

The mailbox lock was frozen. She chipped away at the ice with her keys. It took longer than she expected. It was darker than before. With the package on her hip, she hurried back to the boy. The house's face was hidden behind a vault of fog, behind embankments of snow. She imagined the house chipped away from the cliff, the breaking weight as the wood planks cracked against the ice and stones. She imagined the boy in the window, swallowed whole by the house and torrents. When the woman got back to the river's edge, she waved the package above her head. She smiled her best smile, even though her lips were cracked, her teeth cold. The cardboard package was wrapped in bright pictures of eggs in green-grass baskets, puffy chicks in pickups, a cartoon bunny lying on a rainbow. An entire spring day plucked from fiction.

On the stairs, the woman could not see the boy's red hat. She could not see his dark hair, his big eyes. She heard the river behind her, ice breaking along the lines of hurried chutes. The fog rolled across the snow and ice, transforming the world into a hazy dream—one where the boy was a ghost, and she was a ghost, and both remained unseen.

Glacier

BETTY CULLEY

It creaks along the coast
Slippery fish hatch by its side
A cold stream grows under its belly
as it drags itself,
like a white whale surprised out of sea
by the sounding
of its own insistent tide.

The Legend of Haskell Rock

CHRISTOPHER PACKARD

It is Saturday, June 19, 1841. It's cold, I'm wet, and I am having a very bad day.

"Are you a ghost?" I ask the little man as he climbs up the rock I'm perched on in the middle of the rain-swollen East Branch of the Penobscot River.

"No, sir, I'm not a ghost. Do I look like one?" he replies in a lithe Scottish accent. His voice rings out over the roaring rapids behind us. His cheerful, bright tone offers a welcome relief; the constant roar of the river has been my only companion for hours.

"Well, no," I respond. "It's just that I've been stuck up on this rock for ages, and I can't get across this river back to shore. My crew's gone and left me. And then you come along and just hop across, from log to log, through the white water as if it's nothing. You're not even wet."

"Well, I am a bit on my left pant leg," he concedes, and I see that he is. But I'm soaked and I'm shivering uncontrollably. He continues, "But anyhow, I was curious about your situation. I was wondering what you were doing up here, boyo." He grins at me, and as the sun momentarily emerges from behind a cloud, its rays light up his face, highlighting the friendly puckish twinkle in his eyes. I can't help but smile back. But then, the memory of why I'm here resurfaces, and I remember that I'm shivering atop this giant, gnarled rock pillar in the middle of the river, surrounded by logs crashing by.

"I was working a river drive," I tell him, "and I was breaking up a logjam that had formed right here around this accursed rock." I smack it, and the little pebbles and grit it's made of dig into my hand. I pause at the sensation. He looks at me expectantly, like a child waiting for a story. He's not much taller than a child, but the lines etched around his eyes and the streaks of gray in his hair suggest he's maybe fifty, twice my own age, or more.

"This late river drive has been nothing but trouble. The water is too low, and the logs have been snagging and jamming the whole way since Matagamon. We were all exhausted when we got here. We'd portaged, dragged mostly, the big flat-bottomed bateau over the pitch there behind us. We were supposed to have lunch here, and it was already late. But when we got here, we saw this massive jam. It was all the way across, and wedged on this rock. The water and logs had already begun to build up behind it, and that's the kind of trouble that only gets worse. I knew there would be no lunch for us until this was all sorted. So I ran out with a pike pole and started working on it. I quickly managed to pry a few logs loose, and I slid my pole down under another. But just as the rest of the crew starts climbing out onto the jam, the whole mass lets loose. I lose my footing. And caulk boots be damned, I slip off and hit the water." I pause. The wet wool I'm wearing is suddenly tight, cold, and becoming unbearably itchy and odorous. I feel the uneven surface of the rock dig into my backside.

"And then you climbed up here, did ya?" he prompts.

I think for a second. I can hear the water roaring. I can smell the wet pine logs in the water. My head aches.

"No," I say. "Then I was washed downstream by the torrent; the logs were bumping into me from above, the rocks from below. I reckon I was swept some two-thirds of a mile down. I ended up at the wing dam we'd constructed along the bank to keep the logs from piling up. It was working, but I was stuck in the spin hole, going around and around, and try as I may, I couldn't get a grip on those waterlogged logs of the wing dam to haul myself out. Eventually, a big log hit me hard in the back of the head. Knocked me out. Pushed me under. Next thing I remember I'm pulling myself up out of the river onto this rock."

"You don't say," he whispers as he considers my story. We sit without speaking for a moment, listening to the river, and the wind in the pines. There don't seem to be any more logs coming by; the drive must have ended. The sun's setting now, too.

"That's quite a story there, friend. And some bad luck! Hey," he says with sudden realization, "what's your name, boyo?"

"William M. Haskell, from Poland, out toward Lewiston. Everyone told me not to do this late-season drive. They insisted they were always nothing but trouble. I think they were right." I turn and look at him, "So what's your name?"

"Most folks around these parts call me Sock Saunders." He almost sings his name.

"I've heard people talking about you. You're a bit of a legend, always causing trouble and playing tricks on people. I didn't think you were a real person. Say, you reckon you can help me get off this rock?"

"Ahhhhh now." He sighs. "I would if I could. But I'm much better at getting people into trouble than I am at getting them out of it," he admits with a sigh. He then closes his eyes and scrunches up his face, hard in introspection. His size and this expression make him look like an elf. Suddenly his eyes spring open, he nods vigorously and says, "But don't fret, your brother George and a couple other fellows will be along to get you shortly."

This doesn't make any sense. George is surely back on his own farm in Poland, as it's still planting season. He'd never venture up here, not now. And besides, he was the one that urged me the most not to take this job.

Just as I'm about to say as much, Sock interjects, "You know ... are you certain you're not the one who's the ghost here on Haskell Rock?"

And suddenly, I'm alone again. Stuck on a rock in the East Branch of the Penobscot River, waiting for help.

Notes about the legend:
As far as I know, all the facts in this story are true. The Penobscot River was once the center of a great lumber industry that helped fuel the growth of America. In the 1800s many men sought their fortunes lumbering in the woods, but this was dangerous work. Countless men lost their lives cutting, hauling, and driving logs on and around Maine's great rivers. Most of those who died were buried in the woods and their names forgotten.

William Haskell's body was recovered from the water by his older brother George and two companions some twenty-two days after the jam's break had swept him downstream. William was buried along the shores of the East Branch of the Penobscot River, likely in what is now the Katahdin Woods and Waters National Monument. There, Haskell Rock, an oddly-shaped, twenty-foot-tall conglomerate pillar, and the series of rapids flowing around it still bear his name. Unlike most men who lost their lives in the woods, William Haskell's name is not forgotten.

For some decades, Sock Saunders was a well-known figure in Maine's lumber woods. However, those who knew him best knew that he was not a man. Instead, he was thought to be a mischievous old-world elf who played troublesome and dangerous pranks on the lumberjacks—trees falling the wrong way, log piles collapsing, chain knotting or breaking, fires starting, or any other bit of dangerous bad luck was said to be his doing. In some places, any accident that nearly resulted in injury or death was quickly answered by the lumberjack shouting, "You didn't get me this time, Sock Saunders!"

Beauty Is a Blessing

Gary Rainford

Four sun speckled tree trunks share
one massive, bulging root

system, and where they emerge
from the groundswell

are the thick, angular trapezius
muscles that connect a bodybuilder's neck

to the rest of their body. "This world
is beautiful," sings Nick Cave,

into my headphones, analog synthesizer
shaping birdsong into butterflies

which explode, like confetti,
from a patch of wild daises. I tip my head

back against the shed wall and thank
the clouds for this moment.

Becoming the Food of Stars

Suzanne DeWitt Hall

I wonder if
the tiny stream flowing
in the woods behind our landlocked home
feeds sea stars?
The water from this year's endless rain
traveling through
the drenched dirt of our yard
carrying the juice of rotting leaves
fallen branches
scat and pollen
thistle seeds, berries,
flower petals, feathers
in riotous decomposition.
The stream flows somewhere.
Does it join a larger creek
merge with a tributary
finally reaching the river
which winds to the place
where fresh water meets salt
our immigrant detritus transforming
into food for plankton
plankton for clams
clams for sea stars
a chain of wonder we witness
in rocky pools at low tide?

It's You, It's YOU!!

SARAH CARLSON

I call his name just as I arrive.
He turns, brightens,
runs up the hill from our campsite.
Every so often he throws in a little dance,
repeats over and over,
"Oma! It's you, it's you!!"
The energy of his joy envelops me
as I pick him up for a quick hug,
my heart all aflutter.
Later, as Mama and Dada
head down the Golden Road
to pick up food and supplies,
we share some tent time
and then decide to build a fire, just because.
Together we fan the flames, stoke it a bit, simply sit and watch.
The wind picks up as he climbs onto my lap,
clearly in need of some cuddle time.

I wrap him in his adventure blanket (a.k.a. Blanky)
and quietly sing our song.
He slides gently into sleep just as rain begins to fall.
The soothing sounds of distant whitewater and raindrops on the tarp,
the sweetness of his trust and love,
the soft, dual movement
of the eddy as it flows past our little beach
produce a stirring of my soul
that is deep and primal and needed.
The shifting currents of healing,
though powerful and true, can at times be disorienting.
In these moments along the Penobscot,
and at intervals ever since,
I separate from disquiet,
anchor more securely
to the "you" that he sees,
grateful that it's me.

A Day in the Life of a River Driver

Mary Morton Cowan

Maine rivers have long been important to the lumber industry. For 300 years, the Penobscot River played a major role. Loggers chopped down thousands of trees during the winter months and piled the logs along the riverbank. When ice went out in the spring, men hurled the logs into the water and drove them downriver to sawmills. It was dangerous work, but hundreds of men spent many days like this.

"Can you ride on logs?"

"Sure," you tell the drive boss. He needs more men. And you need work.

"On the drive, days are longer than they were in the woods," he adds, "and the work's vicious. You'll be soakin' wet most o' the time. This ain't no Sunday school!"

You nod.

"And stag them trousers," he warns, "so's your boot calks don't catch."

You look around. All the men look shabby. And you realize all their pants are cut off just below the knees. One lanky guy, named Martti, stands there in his red wool shirt, his thumbs hooked on his grubby suspenders. He helps you stag your pants, then cuts a slit in the arch of your boots just above the sole. "Let ooze out water little bit," he says. "Feet all crack anyhow, but this help."

The boss has been watching the river for days. Today, he roars, "ROLL 'EM!" Dozens of men start dumping logs from the landing into the stream. They lean into their cant dogs and roll logs at a furious pace.

"Tend out here," the drive boss barks at you and some others. "Don't want no logs jammin' up."

You're in and out of the water all morning, poking at logs to keep them flowing. If anyone sits down for a moment, the boss is yelling, "Don't you know how to roll a stick? Keep 'em movin.'"

Martti helps you to shore after one long spell in the water. "Come. Rub legs and jump little bit around," he says. "Make blood to warm." In a few minutes, you head back into the icy stream.

The cookee lugs lunch to you twice during the day. Same meal, over and over—ham, potatoes, baked beans, bread, doughnuts, and strong tea. Just as you are gulping down your seventh doughnut, the boss yells again.

"See them logs startin' to jam by that bank?" he roars, pointing to the far shore. "Get 'em back int' the river, quick! Every damn one of 'em!"

You and four other river drivers jump into the bateau, and the boatman takes you across. He pokes around logs and rocks with his pick pole. You five jump ashore and work feverishly, trudging waist-deep in icy water. You free a few logs with your cant dog.

"Jump in, NOW!" the boatman hollers.

Suddenly, sticks come tumbling over the rapids, crashing over each other, forming a pounding mass of logs. The boss waves furiously to someone upriver. "Stop the logs!" his arms say.

"Jee-e-e-roozlum!" he shrieks, swearing and stomping, before you're even back on shore. "We're gettin' a Lulu of a jam here!"

The boss stares at the jam and yells, "We've gotta chop up that key log. Take turns. I don't want anyone gettin' all tuckered out," he says. "Gotta be able to make a beeline for shore faster 'n lightnin'."

After one river hog gets the notch started, you take your turn. "If you hear that log start to split," the boss says, "by Judas, you run like the bejeepers! When she hauls, she'll go tearin' like thunder."

You make a few swings with your ax and get back safely, but that log mass is starting to rumble. Martti takes his turn next, chopping further into the key log. Before you can blink, the log snaps, releasing a geyser of water. The whole mass goes thrashing and grinding over the rapids, logs upending every which way. Martti can't get back! He leaps onto a log and starts riding it down through. He swivels and turns, dodging rocks like a pro. Suddenly his log rams into a boulder. Head over heels, he is thrown into the raging river.

"Damnation!" the boss cries. "Martti's gone down."

By the big rapids, you bury your buddy in his driving clothes, and hang his calked boots on a tree. He belongs here now. "He died doing his duty," the boss mutters. He scuffs some dirt onto the shallow grave.

Back at the wangan, the cook has a fire blazing, and the big kettle boiling. Bread is baking in the Dutch ovens. You pick at your plate of beans and drink some hot tea. Then you crawl into the lean-to, and plop onto the fir boughs. Some guys don't even take their boots off. Too stiff to put them on in the morning, they say.

All night long, you hear the hollow thunk of logs bumping over the rapids. Like drums. In the morning, you know you'll have more jams.

First Light (Mattawamkeag)

Douglas W. Milliken

My father lays them out on deck boards blanched silver by sun and lake water and immemorial bitter storms. Three rainbow trout, paralleled on wood above the quiet mouth-sounds of water against dock—water stirred only by a feather of breeze and the allure of a moon we can't see—bare inches removed from the liquid home they've always known and will never taste again. Breakfast. Yet looking into the wet mirrors of their alien eyes, I forget these three are not alive, for a moment comprehend the stilled blades of their bodies as the paralyzing awe of, for the first and last time, seeing the sky unfiltered through water's rippling prism, this dim yet glowing nonlight of violet like a filmmaker's trick—like the lateral stripes rainbowing a trout—repeating dizzyingly across the expressionless face of the lake in this first hour before dawn.

Smokestack Down

HANS KRICHELS

Amazing intersection that is
at the corner of School Street and Franklin
in our little town by the river,
with its great paper mill
now shuttered for good.
Looking North:
four church steeples
piercing the clouds overhead.
And down on the waterfront,
three smokestacks,
towering over the old mill site
obelisks in their way—
Priapussian, an elderly woman,
was heard to say.
Her long white hair was drawn into a braid,
and she held the hand of a grandchild.
That was last year, of course,
two years ago, in fact,
and since then
two churches have closed,
steeples crumbling,
sagging through their rooftops.
While down on the millsite
demolition crews have been busy,
and just yesterday,
the last great smokestack came down,
a three hundred and sixty foot wonder,

with blinking jewel at its tip,
warning the planes away.
Until yesterday, of course:
a sharp explosion at the base,
a kneecapping in its way,
and the great stack
thundering to the ground
in a cloud of dust and debris.
Oh woe unto them,
the white-haired woman whispered,
heard only by herself and the child,
emblem of an era
lying limp and lost in the rubble.
While deep beneath the wreckage,
in an old burial site by the river,
aboriginal spirits stirred,
matriarchs gathered,
and a fresh wind
blew across the landscape.
At the corner of School Street and Franklin,
the old woman clutched
the hand of her grandchild, smiled,
and watched the wind swirl,
play on the water,
and sweep away the cloud of dust
that shrouded the rubble.

Penobscot River Rock

CHRISTOPHER C.C. LEE

There once was a poet who wrote about the impatience of a stone waiting to be ground down and become part of something that was alive, for better or worse. All along the Penobscot River, water grinds down minerals from 400-million-year-old stones.

David hauled the bucket out of the river and sloshed the mana into the irrigation trough to water his snap peas. He chewed on a snap pea he had picked and imagined that the minerals from the stones upriver would flow into his muscles; it was sweet and crispy. David dropped the bucket, his eyes beaded on something white shooting down the Penobscot. He jumped into the river, felt it pulling at his legs, warning him to not come in. He climbed out, sprinted to the canoe, pushing it to danger awaiting and jumped in; David wanted to grab the milk bottle before it passed by his house. "Damn them! Throwing garbage in the river."

He raced out to intercept the bottle as it shot toward him, then past him and away from him. He dug deep with his paddle, too deep; the river grabbed the wood and pulled him under.

David Junior climbed into grandma's lap. "Again," he said.

"What's the magic word?" asked grandma.

"Please," he smiled, batting his long eyelashes.

"You are so cute!" Grandma hugged him, like a bear if she could, but she was of small bones and stature, so she squeezed as hard as she could. She bounced three-year-old Junior on her lap and sang his favorite songs.

"Junior. You know you're too big for that now," scolded Michelle. "Here, Grandma," she said, handing her bottled water. "You must be thirsty after all that bouncing."

"I am, but you know Junior is going to be grown up before I can bat an eyelash. Got to enjoy what I can now, while I can. Where's David?"

"Your son is babying his vegetables again. Hauling water from the river because it gives life, he says. Should be in soon."

Junior played with grandma for a while.

"Lunch, Mom?"

"Soon. Go find Daddy and ask him to pick some snap peas for lunch. Take Grandma with you," said Michelle.

"Ok! Come, Grandma."

They skipped out to find Daddy, and Grandma threw the empty plastic water bottle in the kitchen garbage.

Michelle saw her. She would have to show David what his mother just did.

A boat puttered up to the shore, an upside down canoe in tow. David sat huddled in a blanket, shivering. The helm waved back at Junior; she wore a khaki uniform and her hair in a bun under a cap. She shifted the engine into neutral and guided the bow onto the sand.

"Daddy!" yelled Junior.

David jumped out of the boat, his hoodie dripping wet. Shivering, he pulled at the mooring line and secured it to a rusting, ancient plow.

"What happened, David?" asked Grandma.

"Just a little accident," replied David.

"Who's this?" asked Junior.

"This is Lauralee. She's a river ranger."

Lunch was without snap peas and laden with awkward conversation; David was brooding and Lauralee tried to make small talk.

"Why did you do that, Mom?" blurted David.

"Do what?"

"Totally mess with what I believe in."

"What?"

"You threw the plastic bottle into the trash. Recycle! I keep telling you!"

"I'm sorry. I was in a rush. I had Junior with me and—"

"Don't blame Junior! You just don't care. You and all the rest of the people in this world. Get out of my house!"

Lauralee grimaced, staring at her food and Michelle cleared her throat. David stomped out.

"I think I better be going," said Lauralee.

As Lauralee climbed into the boat, the river lapped at her feet. She paused, realizing that the mooring line was still grounded.

"I'll get that," yelled David.

"Hold on, David," replied Lauralee. "You have great concern for the environment, don't you?"

David looked down, holding the mooring line. It wasn't his fault he got angry.

"We have a community awareness program we could use some help on."

"I don't like crowds," he replied.

"Well, it's not like a lot of people come to these public events. David, I'd like to show you something we are very proud of."

"Sorry, I've got—," replied David.

"I'm not taking no for an answer, David. I picked you out of the river. You owe me one."

The clouds were turning dark, so Lauralee accelerated. The noise of the engine made conversation difficult, which both of them were grateful for. Lauralee hoped David would get what his soul needed. She had seen much change in the river since 1999. It had looked like a very angry river or maybe, she thought, the anger was hers. Now the river seemed to play with her, like an otter, bringing people like David to her.

"Look! Over there!" she pointed.

A silver salmon jumped and splashed, then another, flashes in the water, all heading toward a concrete pool by the dam.

"Atlantic salmon. Endangered," she shouted. "With this fish elevator to help them upriver, they're making a comeback."

"I'm glad to see conservationists, finally, have power to do something," he replied.

"That's not where the power came from. David, it took an entire tribal nation, seven conservation groups, a power company, the federal government, and the people of Maine to make this happen. A lot of people, David. A lot of good people working to make this a better world."

David avoided her eyes. He knew she was quoting the words he used against his mother.

"I think you would like volunteering with us. You get to change the way things are."

"Well, you shouldn't rest on your laurels. People are people; they will break this all down, if you let them," he replied.

Lauralee sucked back anger; she turned the boat quickly, sending up spray and slamming David into the port side. He grabbed for something to keep from falling over.

"Sorry, David. You all right?"

"Yes, yes."

"We could use volunteers, David."

"Sorry, too busy. Kid and all, you know."

The ride back to the house was quiet. David stared at the water. He had invited his mother to come and see her first grandson a few months after he was born; it was a difficult trip for her so they had decided to delay until Junior was old enough to remember the visit.

"I'm sorry about blowing up like that," he said.

"You lost your canoe," she replied, "nearly drowned. You're just stressed out."

As the boat approached the shore, he turned to her. "About that volunteer job?" he said.

At dinner, there were snap peas and laughter as David reminisced with his mother about embarrassing moments when he was growing up. Junior crammed the sweetness of the snap peas into his mouth, the minerals from the stones becoming a slurry with his saliva, dripping down his chin.

"Junior," said Michelle, wiping Junior's mouth. "Close your mouth when you eat."

Junior chewed and mumbled about Grandma and him painting a river stone, a gift from Lauralee.

When All Is Right Here, the Fish Return

Kara Douglas

The river sings its invitation, streaking its scent across the sea.
From the salty expanse they surface,
alewives, American shad, blueback herring,
moving out of depth and darkness
toward water that runs quick and clear.

Resilient, they turn toward the cold current,
sensing the way, navigating simultaneously,
the future and the past, generations
of instinct and adaptation,
onward, onward.

Before the great forgetting, they were celebrated,
heralded, known for the life they carried and spawned.
All night, I dream of them,
silver brilliance of scales and water spray,
their able bodies hurtling homeward.

Something in the Water

SHANE LAYMAN

There was something in the water; that's what the old timers used to say. At least, that's what they used to say before things completely fell apart. But that wasn't entirely accurate. What they were referring to was just below the water, resting dormant deep in the muddy riverbed, quietly biding its time, patiently waiting for the opportunity to show humankind just how small it truly was in this world.

When Earth's atmospheric temperature began to steadily climb, it would become clear that not enough people showed cause for concern. The good people of Maine would learn, regrettably, that when the smaller lakes and rivers started running dry, too many red flags were ignored. Even when the mighty Penobscot River dropped nearly three feet in one summer, concern seemed lackluster at best. It wasn't until *they* started clawing and crawling their way out of the murky depths of the newly exposed riverbed that any real attention was paid.

And by then, of course, it was far too late.

For thousands of years, the Penobscot River was the beating heart of Maine— the life vein for generations of Indigenous Peoples who populated the land long before European settlers landed on the eastern shores of North America. Later, the smaller rivers, lakes, and streams that were fed by the Penobscot would provide the water needed for generations of farm families. It was used to transport millions of tons of trees from northern Maine all the way down to the Penobscot Bay, where the river bled out into the ocean. From there, the lumber was bought and sold all over the world. Any student worth their salt didn't get through middle school history in Maine without knowing and understanding the impact that the lumber industry had on the financial success of Maine's economy, all of which would have been nearly impossible without the aid and blessing of the river itself.

Ironically, the beneficial impact that the Penobscot River had on the people and economy of Maine would be historically and grossly overshadowed by the fact that the river itself would play the most critical role in the state's devastating collapse. Dubiously, the river was hiding one tiny, deadly little secret.

Those few who had shown concern in the early years focused on the fact that average temperatures were increasing all over the planet. Not a lot, a tenth of a degree one year and a half a degree another year—just small enough for skeptics to break out their sunscreen and swim trunks and tell anyone willing to listen that we should embrace the warmth, go to the lake more often. What's a few degrees in the grand scheme of things?

Slowly and persistently, those few degrees started to increase, as those who predicted such things assumed would happen. Coral reefs started dying off en masse. Forest fires ravaged normally damp woodlands. Humankind marveled in awe that heat records were being broken all over the planet. But what could humans do?

More sunscreen!

More time at the lake!

But by then, even the lakes were beginning to recede. Water levels were setting their own records—not for how warm they had become but for how low they had receded.

At about the same time, scientists were concerned that permafrost in parts of China and Russia was beginning to soften. Their concern, while legitimate, was misguided. The softening and hardening of permafrost had occurred countless times over the planet's long life span. It wasn't the permafrost that should have concerned the scientists as much as what lay within the permafrost. Thousands of bacteria and viruses lay dormant in the frozen ground not seen by humankind in centuries, millennia in some instances. Some viruses and bacteria humans of that time had never seen before and so, naturally, had no knowledge of, no immunity to, and, most imperatively, no vaccine for.

The Penobscot, like the thawing, decaying permafrost, shared the same dirty little secret.

The virus that reanimated the first bodies that had been buried in the bed of the Penobscot River would never actually be known to humankind. There would be no time for research. No time to develop vaccines. There wouldn't really even be time to defend themselves.

There would be dozens of corpses unwittingly awakened from the dark depths of death all up and down the length of the Penobscot River that day. The first body to crawl out of the mucky sludge belonged to Philip Novak, a local fisherman who was illegally fishing for elvers in the early morning hours of April 15, 1982. Attending to his gear, not paying attention to where he was on the river, his little dinghy hit a large rock hiding just underneath the surface of the water. In the darkness, Philip never saw the rock. When the boat tipped over, he tried desperately to right the vessel and climb back in, but the temperature of the water was dangerously frigid and Philip began to lose functioning in his fingers. Within a minute, he had lost feeling in the rest of his body. Since he wasn't wearing a life jacket, his frozen body sank into the icy water at 3:22 a.m. and never resurfaced. The little boat was discovered by Search and Rescue six miles down the river. With such a large search area, local authorities never stood a chance of finding the body.

Of course, the body that crawled out of the mud was nothing like the one that sank into it. On the morning Philip's body sank to the bottom of the river, his upper body must have snagged on a downed tree and then submerged in mud because the torso and head were remarkably preserved—looking nothing like the Philip who went into the water, of course. The long, dark hair, which he kept in a ponytail, was now matted and clumped together, clinging to his face like a bloated starfish. His eyes were drained of color and resembled the murky water from which he had emerged. The lower body, however, had been picked clean by scavengers over the decades, leaving nothing but exposed bone from the waist down, which made standing impossible. Instead, Philip—or the body that was Philip—continued to crawl, arm over arm, toward the river's edge. With no ability to stand or walk, this decomposed body struggled to squirm and wriggle toward land.

Something inside was driving this mindless, rotting body forward—an unexplainable, undeniable urge.

Shelly Taylor, who had sat down on the grassy bank of the river, was going to enjoy a beautiful day. It was a Saturday, her only day off that week. She had decided she would have a picnic by the water and read a book. Shelly had had the terrible misfortune of falling asleep while reading. A copy of *Pride and Prejudice and Zombies* lay open on her stomach as Philip, the real zombie, made landfall. With no one nearby to warn poor Shelly of her impending doom, she was helpless to stop Philip as he grabbed her foot and sank yellow, rotting teeth into the flesh of her leg. As one would suppose, Shelly screamed bloody murder. She kicked at what seemed to be impossible: a man with only half a body—an upper torso connected to what looked like a gross parody of those skeletons that were always hanging in corners of high school biology classrooms—was holding on to her ankle with superhuman strength and gnawing her leg as though it was an ear of corn. She continued to kick and scream but this thing, which she assumed had to be a person at some point in time, was abnormally strong. Using the strength of his upper body and his unhinged desire to feed, Philip pulled his whole body up closer to Shelly's stomach where the attack became almost too gruesome to share.

Hearing the screams, a few bold citizens ran to help. However, by the time they arrived on the scene, Philip had consumed most of Shelly's insides and, mercifully, she was no longer screaming. One man in the group, Daniel Day, had ordered the others to go for help. He would investigate. And we know how these things end.

By the time the concerned citizens had returned with the police and local EMTs, there was no sign of the rotting corpse that had clearly been eating Shelly. There was no sign of Shelly, either—no bones, no leftover tidbits. There was nothing but a pool of blood-stained grass and mud. And while the citizens insisted that a man had gone over to check on the situation, there was no sign of him, either.

Investigators would never determine what happened. Unbeknownst to the residents of Maine, this incident involving three individuals was the precursor to a series of attacks that would unfold across the state on that serene Saturday. As for Shelly and Daniel, they reanimated and parted ways, ambling off into the wooded area not too far from where the original attacks had occurred. They would follow their own undeniable urge to feed.

For weeks, people and pets were reported missing on local newscasts with no leads. They had simply vanished.

It wasn't until hordes of zombies converged on cities and towns all over the state, looking for just one thing, that people began to realize what was going on. It wasn't long before hundreds of zombies became thousands of zombies and, within hours, thousands became tens of thousands. Their exponential growth was staggering. Those who were left behind fought desperately for their lives.

But by then, it was far too late.

Penobscot, West Branch, in January

MC MOELLER

We stood on the bank
in our snowshoes.

Is this the place to cross?
A heavy crust of ice and snow,
thick enough to trust?

Come slow, come close, listen and hear
of woodland elk chased into the current,
hunting parties, arrows whistling,
a skull with antlers washed in sand.
Of silver splashes, bending rods and fighting fish,
eagles diving with talons spread.
Of ice dams flooding settler cabins,
loaded wagons overturned, the horses drowned.
Of log rafts miles long waiting,
downstream the saw blades scream.
Of iron-sided barges and girded bridges.

Our footsteps leave their mark
on river and rock, as they left theirs,
men who lived by deer hide,
men who lived by lumber,
men who lived by steel.

Water roars and water whispers,
the river does not sleep.
While we breathe, we assemble memories.
Come close, listen to the river.

Full Chorus

JEAN ANNE FELDEISEN

This snowstorm
> a cantata
> for mixed forest
blows between dark
> timbre of tree trunks
in staccato tones
> of icy light
> fresh orchestration for
darting birds
> dancing branches
seen   clearly
> against white.
Flakes fly
> sideways
> in cadenced gusts.
Accents of
> snow clumps
> drop
> in soft-pedaled
> thumps.
The music swirls
> howls
> in crescendo
> then dies away.
Again
> and again.
> Hallelujah!
Hallelujah!
> Conducted by
> a master wind.

Lucky Streak

LESLIE MOORE

Mid-March. The big nor'easter spits
       a mere two inches of snow overnight.
Winter's last wheeze.

The city plow growls down Huntress Ave.,
       groans back up again, spewing
a fantail of Peruvian salt.

Now a yellow Lab gallops past—
       head high, ears sailing,
no owner in sight.

I lean out the door and whistle,
       but there's no stopping the dog.
Penobscot Bay beckons

at the foot of our street. Her tail
       flickers like flames
in dim morning light.

This girl's not going to let
       a grizzle of snow get in her way.
She's free and she's having fun!

I'm going to tug on boots and race
       down the street after her,
bathrobe flapping behind me.

At the Water's Edge

SARAH WALKER CARON

It's dusk when I arrive, gravel-littered asphalt crunching beneath my tires on the warm July evening. I've been thinking about this moment for hours—all day really—when I could roll back from my desk, pack up, and drive to the water.

It calls to me. It always has.

From my car, I pull the striped chair, neon cooler, and canvas bag. I leave my inner tube—there will be no swimming today; it's too deserted. Then I make my way past my car, across the grass, toward the water's edge.

I'm here. I'm finally here.

Baby-blue and powder-pink ribbons spread across the sky, blending together in places—a calming watercolor. The sun is low, dipping beneath trees at the far end of the lake. Usually I come midday, when I am not working, and the sun casts a warm gaze across everything. But not this time. It's too late.

I don't care. I want to be here.

In my haste to get here, I hadn't considered the sun. It's still out, but too low to cast the warm gaze it does when I come midday. It's not as I pictured. Not exactly. I open my chair anyway, stretching the fabric and then clicking the chair back into place. It's still light and will be for hours.

I gaze at the water. I need this.

My grandmother used to say that we should let the water wash away our troubles. She meant the salty tidal waves of the Long Island Sound, but I've found that any water will do. I can breathe in the calm as I walk along the Penobscot River or sit by Pushaw Lake, releasing the stress that nips at my shoulders and muddles my thoughts.

I'm drawn to this. I'm happy to be here.

Staring out across the glassy surface with the grass beneath my toes, everything begins to make sense again. I gulp in inner peace, greedy for its quieting.

At the water's edge, I am home.

Life and the Day

JAMES BRASFIELD

The day's chill remains,
though the poplar's spring catkins
drop from leaves.

The Penobscot has been ever as it is,
though I've not seen the river frozen.
Wavelets, rough now, define

its current. After watching it for hours
I've come inside, built a fire,
spare as it is in the hearth.

Fog in from the bay
was like another night falling,
overlapping the dark.

Close by, beyond the pines,
a freight train is passing,
from where to where? ...

that darkness, that darkness—
this room my domain for a time,

wind will take care of the dead branches.

Riverine

Shannon Bowring

I.

This September morning, I sit by the river. Sunlight filters through pale green and yellow leaves. The sky is cornflower blue; the breeze smells like cold water, ripe apples. Only a few people walk or bike past my sheltered spot at the base of a granite sculpture, whose stone chills me and supports me all at once.

There is no purpose for me to be beside the river other than that I woke up this morning and felt a quiet yet urgent need to be here. I have heard and answered this call often since X left. Sometimes I think this river has taken his place. Given me the companionship I desperately crave yet don't feel entitled to.

X and I broke up this past spring, and I still feel a stabbing loneliness in my chest each time I return alone to the apartment we once shared. I redecorated after he left, swapping movie posters for bland renderings of flowers and beaches. Filling the empty spaces on the bookshelves with paperbacks from Goodwill. Ridding myself of the lumpy couch and accepting my parents' gift of a coffee-colored, foldout loveseat. I feel like a prisoner in a jail I have constructed myself, one made of department-store art and books I may never read. All held together with the gritty mortar of regret.

I am not a woman scorned; I am the woman who did the scorning. The end would have come eventually—we were too young; we wanted too many different things—but I hastened that ending and made it far worse than it had to be. Acted selfishly, caused pain. I am only twenty-three, and I know nothing, but I should have known better than that.

These past few months, as I navigate life as a single person, only a few things have kept me partly sane: writing, walking, and the river. I have poured my remorse onto the pages of my journal, pounded my feet against the sidewalks of familiar streets as the sun sinks low and turns the earth gold, pondered my wickedness as blue currents float beyond me, to places I will never go.

I used to tell X that I would be a river. It was part of a game we'd been playing since we were teenagers. *If you were a vegetable, what would you be? Baby carrot. If you were a tree? Elm. Body of water? River.* The other answers changed—sometimes I imagined myself more of a clementine or a weeping willow—but it was always river. "Why?" X would ask, and I'd tell him I loved how rivers were the same but also constantly changing, different every second, minute shifts in pattern, speed, flow beneath the current. Rivers were always where you left them, yet they never stopped moving. Sometimes placid; sometimes wild. Even the color was never quite the same—green in one light, gray or blue in another—and I loved that poetic sort of moment-by-moment transformation. The infinite possibility.

This fall morning, as I stare out over the water flowing past me, my mind hums with words. I remember what I was writing in my journal before I left my apartment to walk down here, thoughts about painful endings and what can and cannot be forgiven. I've had a crisis of faith these past few months, not in the world but in myself. I used to think I was a good person. I don't think that anymore. Remarkable, how unpoetic an affair actually is, how paltry and tedious. Bleak.

Despite everything I have done and everything I have lost, though, I still believe in poetry, and in words—their own infinite possibility, their power to bring both writer and reader to life. Words and stories are transformative magic, mirrors that reflect not only who we have been and who we are, but who we are capable of one day becoming. And words have been my saving grace since X left, the life raft I have clung to with white-knuckled desperation. I write of the bad things I have done, and the ways I might redeem myself. The ways I might transform, minutely, moment-by-moment, beneath the surface.

If you are a river, can you baptize yourself? Use your own current to wash away the dirt and the hurt, make yourself clean once again?

This river at my feet is not meant for any sort of baptism. I've heard stories of the pollution here, the poison that has lingered long after the initial contamination from lumberyard, textile mill, thoughtless human waste. Invisible toxicity.

If you look at it just right, the statue I rest upon this morning is meant to resemble a watchtower. The cold, hard granite is comforting, but not comfortable.

The stone says nothing, yet it reverberates with all the words I might write after I leave the river, pen poised and aimed like a dagger toward the white blank page.

II.

It feels good to be alone in my own bed this May morning, to wake with only the sun beside me. I lie still yet restless in the light, dreading the drudgery that waits for me at the therapists' office where I perform quality analysis on client charts for eight hours a day in a basement that smells like mildew. There's one small window on the wall above my desk, situated under stairs that lead into the building. All day, I hear footsteps trudging up and down those steps, see stranger-shaped shadows flitting on the ceiling. There are no bars on the window, but there might as well be.

Between scanning paperwork for state-required progress notes and treatment plans, I answer phones, schedule appointments, fill in at the front desk to check clients in and out. Sometimes I can't help but watch these clients in the waiting room and imagine what they will discuss with their therapists. Whether their lives are a whirl of turmoil or a stagnant pool of same, same, same. I wonder about the thin line that separates me from them, whether I should be the one sitting on those unforgiving plastic chairs, hoping someone wise and kind and gentle will bring me into their soothingly lit office and help me answer the big questions: How to live. Who to love. What to do. Who to be.

If I listen closely as I lie under my blankets, I might be able to hear M on the other side of the shared wall of our apartment building. I imagine him moving through his familiar kitchen in all his familiar ways. Maybe he will pause, press his ear to his wall, wait to hear me in my apartment and imagine me moving through my rooms, too. Except he doesn't know my morning routine. I always perform it away from him, after I have left his bed and come back here to my own place.

Waking up there, beside him, is a gut-twisting hangover of junk food and other bad decisions. Something akin to punishment. Waking up here, in my own space, is a luxury, a break from penance. And this morning, what I want—what I need—is to hold onto that gift of serene aloneness, unwrap it slowly underneath the sky.

So I call out sick. Migraine. Because if I ask for a mental health day from the therapy office where I work, my boss will say no. But today is for *yes*. Today is for me. Today is for the river.

It's a cool day, fine silver light over everything, aroma of budding leaves floating on the air. In the woods by the river, I follow a trail through bushes and saplings down to a boulder jutting into the water, where tiny whirlpools swirl. Across the river, a brush fire burns, smoke spiraling up into the sky. The acrid smell reaches me here; when I inhale, I imagine my breath glowing inside my lungs, burning like the pot I often smoke with M.

He has pale eyes, nice hands, a way of smirking that can either make me feel infuriated or euphoric, depending on the circumstances. He makes me laugh often, but the air between us is usually rife with tension; he can't make up his mind to keep me close or push me away. Dramatic fights, tear-filled text exchanges.

Living in the same apartment complex as M is swoon-worthy when all is good and only a short walk separates us—nightmarish when we are in an *off-again* stage and I run into him in the parking lot. I am constantly seeking his approval, or maybe his disapproval is what I'm after, further validation that I am a wicked person for what I did to X last year. Maybe disapproval and discontent is what I deserve.

For several weeks now, though, I have been thinking I might have served my sentence. Thinking it might be time to tunnel my way through the walls, squeeze out through that tiny window, bust the glass to emerge blinking and raw in some new, unfamiliar place. Make a run for it, no looking back.

All my life, but especially this past year, I have been plagued by inertia, the desire to stay rooted in one place because it is safer, easier, more convenient. The elm tree standing alone in a field. The weeping willow bound to the watery lands that feed it.

But what about the river? Wasn't I supposed to be a river?

A river takes on toxins and inflicts its own damage, yet keeps on flowing to other rivers, lakes, seas—touched by hurt, transformed by it, but never stopping to linger inside it. A river is always moving forward, toward something distant and unknown, something greater.

I lose track of how long I stand on this private shore and gaze at this river, shifting green to blue, blue to green. Maybe it's fifteen minutes; maybe it's an hour. All I know, all that matters, is that when I emerge from the shadows of the forest, taking the leaf-littered path back into the sun, I have made a decision.

I will leave this place—this town, this job, this not-quite-relationship, this apartment. I don't yet know how, or when, or where I will end up, but I will figure it out. I am only twenty-three, and I know enough to keep moving. Like the river.

Like the river, follow a winding course. Like the river, absorb the light, reflect the sky, hold the memory of everywhere I've been, all the waters I have known—the clean and the tainted, the pure and the dark—and keep flowing onward into all the waters that wait for me, downstream.

White Canvas, by Thomas

J.D. MANKOWSKI

From the exterior, it looked as though Thomas had allowed his home to willingly fall into disrepair. Some of the siding was cracked or missing, shingles littered his unkempt lawn, and the front porch that faced the road had rotted and collapsed.

Thomas was a painter. He wasn't particularly successful, partly because he never sold his work. The people in town knew him to be somewhat of a recluse who dabbled in art, and in his obituary, they would state that he painted the Penobscot with some regularity—which was, in truth, a grotesque understatement.

The inside of Thomas's house was an overcrowded shrine to the river. Every inch of the wall space was a tribute to the water, detailing decades of his observations. Overdue library books were stacked on every table and spare chair, explaining the history, the flora, and the fauna of the region. Dozens of pages were earmarked with margins subsequently sketched in. Others had pressed flowers, preserved for reference in the winter months.

A summer sun rose one fair morning as Thomas set off to paint the river yet again. He was a peculiar figure, with a shock of unruly white hair that danced atop his head. His eyes, worn with age, still held the same glimmer of adventure from his youth. But Thomas couldn't carry much—a standing easel made from pine, a backpack for paint tubes, brushes, a palette, and in a separate pocket, a ham and cheese sandwich.

Memories fluttered across Thomas's thoughts like butterflies, starting with the earliest days of his youth as he hiked over dirt, roots, and stone. He passed an old dock where he and his father used to fish on Sundays. His father had never been particularly religious, but he swore every day up until his last that God had rested on the seventh day in that very spot.

Thomas paused to study hornwort and ditchmoss growing along the river's edge. He listened to the pickerel frogs croak and thought about the ones he used to catch. Many critters of the Penobscot had been temporarily held for observation by his net—snails, snapping turtles, and salamanders. He always released them before returning home, never understanding why the other boys his age tried to jar them up and keep them as pets.

Wading through dense fern groves, Thomas looked up to reminisce about the oaks and maples he used to climb. What he wouldn't give to experience the bliss of running away from the schoolhouse to skip rocks and smoke stolen cigarettes with friends one last time. The great American frontier was their backyard; never did they dream of trying to tame it.

Thoughts like that explained how Thomas fell in love with Beth. And why, not far from where he walked, she had said yes when he proposed to her with nothing more than a stem from an annual daisy fleabane.

Thomas painted the lupines every June in memory of her. He tried to capture their deeper purple shades, and the way they glistened after being caught in a steady rain. Time's cruel decree had dimmed his once keen eyes and steady hand. His most recent lupine painting had been a point of frustration, so much so that it now lay face down on the floor in his garage.

Like the Penobscot he once knew, Thomas found himself in the twilight of his existence. He couldn't hike as far as he wanted. He couldn't reach the areas of the river he still recognized—the areas he so desperately wanted to capture.

Car bridges had sprouted like weeds to the south. Powerlines came shortly after, spanning the river like black webs made by the arachnid pests of industry. Bears had become scarce in areas where they used to hunt. Moose crossed rapids further and further north with the calves. The unnatural buzzing of a future world had marred the peace once found in the past and present.

And yet, for all the noise and nuisance, it was the specter of his final perfect masterpiece that haunted Thomas most. The doctors said he didn't have long—not with the tumor in his brain being inoperable. Only bad songs came from their computers, scanners, and probes. Unlike his muse, who played the sounds of water rolling over stones.

With his focus set on a section of the river, unoccupied by gauche residential homes or defunct paper mills, Thomas prepared to paint. Breathing in deeply, he waited for his canvas to show him the river's gentle current. This canvas was shy. Thomas picked up a pencil to bring forth the ridges and lines of the landscape instead. But again, his blank slate didn't feel ready. Rummaging through his bag for tubes of paint, he held each one up toward the morning sun. It was never too early to plan how he might layer colors so that life could lift off the surface more vibrantly. A sharp ache announced itself above Thomas's right eye.

"No," he thought in frustration. "None of these greens will do."

Six shades of green had been packed, and none of them appropriately mimicked the lush vegetation, towering pines, and foliage embracing the river's shores. This realization led Thomas to then question his selection of blues for the sky, and silvery grays for the water. Maybe he wasn't meant to paint the river in the summer. Maybe he needed to capture how it would look in autumn. On and on Thomas's mind rebelled until finally he stepped away from his easel.

"What a beautiful morning," called a hiker from a short distance away.

Thomas reckoned his ears were going as quickly as his eyes. He had not heard the hiker approaching. "It is," he answered.

"I see you've set yourself up with a perfect view."

"Yup," Thomas replied, hoping the man would not venture closer. He knew his type well, with their long hair, thick glasses, and fancy camping gear—chatty.

"Are you a painter?"

"Nope."

The hiker walked closer, eyeing the blank canvas. "Are you sure?"

"Yup."

Nodding, the hiker then reached into their pocket and pulled out a phone. A crumpled foil wrapper fell to the ground. They brashly thumbed the screen of their device, standing between Thomas's canvas and the water's edge. The hiker snapped a photo, admired it for a moment, and then tucked the phone away.

"I love that old mill there. It's so creepy," the hiker said, pointing one out in the distance.

"A lot of good people had to move when it shut down. The company that polluted our river found it cheaper to import pulp from other countries."

"Oh."

Thomas grunted.

The hiker made an awkward gesture toward the hiking trail behind them after taking Thomas's hint. Finally, they walked away.

Thomas picked up the trash the hiker left behind before taking a seat against one of the birch trees near the water. His own possessions remained laid out behind. Fatigue latched onto him quicker these days. It commonly came on the heels of his unending headache. The doctor had mentioned something about taking prescribed medications in a timely manner, but that would have required

Thomas to pick them up at the local pharmacy—something he refused to do. Like all other earthly pains, he knew this headache too would subside. Being among nature was healing; swallowing pills just temporarily pacified problems.

Through the clearing between two trees Thomas looked across the river at the opposite bank. It was raised on a wall of exposed granite. The majestic tops of pine trees rocked in an unfelt breeze. Here and there herons and egrets swooped in search of fish. And further back, there rose the deeper mountain woods and glens that framed the lowest reaches of the sky. Cow-spotted by shadows made under cumulus clouds, the natural splendor of places he had never been and never would go kept stretching.

The empty canvas continued to haunt Thomas. His majestic muse remained elusive. He ate his sandwich to pass more time. Patience was a painter's best companion, or so one of his overdue library books once professed.

For some time, Thomas sat, admiring this scene; the afternoon gradually passed him; the shade from his painting spot spilled out onto the river. His ears picked up a high-pitched tone that emphasized his headache. It hurt for a moment. So much so that he inhaled a deep breath to try to calm himself. Then it stopped all at once for the cry of a solitary raven winging its way from a tree nearby.

A small cluster of maple leaves peeked out from a sea of green. Crisp air from the north tagged along behind the sweeter scent of phlox flowers. Geese announced their departure for fields closer to the equator.

Gray skies moved overhead. They swept away the summer's warmth and brought with it a stronger wind. Thomas heard his easel tip. He would have gotten up to fix it, but his fatigue told him to worry about it later. His head wasn't aching for the moment, and there were small chanterelle mushrooms breaking free from a log that needed his attention.

It was difficult to tell if the evening was fast approaching with the sun being blocked. Thomas contemplated going home, but the dried leaves rustling in the wind recommended that he should stay put just a bit longer. A few maple leaves fell free from above him to offer their jewel tones of red, yellow, and orange as inspiration for his painting. Who was he to ignore them? Thomas studied each one with care before tucking them into the chest pocket of his fleece for safe keeping.

Only after he turned around did Thomas realize that his canvas and easel were missing. They hadn't been stolen; they were merely lost beneath a heavy blanket of snow. He would have to wait until spring to find them. It didn't matter. Of all the seasons, winter was his favorite. It forced him to miss all the others—their scents, colors, and sounds. It forced him to miss the river.

Thomas could hear the deep groan and creaking of shifting ice. It was the only proof that the water was still there. Everything above it was under the cyclical spell of an ancient slumber. Only the eyes of aspens remained vigilant in witnessing the long, dark nights. Not even Thomas could fight the lullaby of snow falling softly from the heavens above; the flecks of ice being spun up by a rapid wind; the soft patter of a snow hare on the move; the heavy thud of spruce trees shedding their white coats.

Then all at once it was spring again, and Thomas knew what he was going to paint. He was going to paint it all, every color of every season all at once. He had spent years trying to capture moments in time, never nature's blinding essence. His spirit rose with the dandelions and clover. His excitement buzzed with the first flight of the bees. Thomas painted everything, starting with the body he left behind, nestled among the lupines in June.

Confluence

CATHERINE J.S. LEE

Have you seen me
flowing from the meeting
of North Branch and South Branch,
spilling out of Seboomook Dam,
raising mist above the facets of slate-dark ledge
into the heart-shaped leaves of quaking aspen?

Have you seen me
rushing through the steep and foliage-flocked canyon
of Ripogenus Gorge,
my waters white as cumulus clouds,
roaring like a dozen waterfalls
over the multitude of rocks and boulders?

Have you seen me,
West and East Branches joined,
leaving behind the forested wilderness,
running broad and majestically through river towns,
past camps and fallow farmlands,
to reach my journey's end in the wide and teeming sea?

And have you seen me,
one small writer scribbling in a worn notebook,
breathing in the aromas of pine and clean water,
trying to get the details down
as the unending and ever-changing current
carries mind and heart beyond myself
into oneness?

Of Wolves and Sharks

RET TALBOT

By the time the Penobscot River enters Penobscot Bay, by the time as much as 13,000 cubic feet per second of water gleaned from a watershed of over 20,000 square kilometers passes Eddington above Bangor, by the time the upsurge of the tidal swell greets the weight of fresh water and recedes back under the Penobscot Narrows Bridge—by then it's too late. Those specific molecules of water, that hydrogen and oxygen churned into one of the planet's greatest forces, have ceased to be what they once were. Daily, they've mingled with 150 million gallons of wastewater and accumulated chlorinated organics, chromium, copper, dioxin, lead, vanadium, zinc ... the list goes on. Where once salmon runs numbered in the tens of thousands and sustained the Penobscot Nation along with shad and sturgeon for more than 8,000 years, today's Penobscot people live on land stolen from them and degraded by 400 years of progress yielding the need for "Penobscot River Fish Consumption Advisories" for mercury, PCBs, and dioxins.

I sit on a beach on First Debsconeag Lake just a short paddle from where the West Branch of the Penobscot swells below Debsconeag Falls into a lazy dead-water over which Mount Katahdin stands sentinel. The campfire snaps like twigs breaking beneath the hoof of a bull moose on a cold October morning—when frost encapsulates the remnant green on grass blades awaiting the low-slung angle of the sun to perhaps free them for one more day before the crush of winter. The embers blaze. The lake is still. Afterglow turns the color of squid ink. I hear a howl coming from somewhere beyond the fire's glow—from somewhere deep in the forest or perhaps from an exposed rib of granite where a dog-like animal is silhouetted against the night. I try hard to imagine that the high pitch howl I hear is the deeper bass of a wolf, but I know it is not. It's a coyote, or as some may claim, a coywolf—a hybrid animal undefined by wildlife managers, debated by taxonomists, and killed on sight by many hunters because it is viewed as a competitor. The howl dissolves into a staccato—a series of distinctly high-pitched calls best described as yelps. It's impossible to imagine a wolf here. The Penobscot River passes by undeterred, its dark waters bedazzled by the reflection of constellations. I hear the howl again ... still imagining.

My mind travels many miles downstream and a short way into Penobscot Bay, where chicken factories once lined Belfast's waterfront. It's said white sharks were attracted to the blood and viscera heaving with the ebb tide like a feather-strewn chum slick stretching out across the bay toward the Atlantic. The chicken factories are now gone, and with them, so too went the sharks, but not just from Penobscot Bay. The white shark population in the western North Atlantic declined precipitously with the extirpation of seals thanks to decades of state-sanctioned bounties. Along the Massachusetts coast, a seal hunter could produce a seal tail or the nose along with its skin, and the town clerk would pay the hunter as much as five dollars. The first seal bounty in Maine was restricted to the Penobscot River and Bay, where a seal nose alone was rewarded with fifty cents. Soon the bounty was expanded to the entire state of Maine and the price increased to a dollar. As many as 135,000 seals were killed on the coast of New England. Maybe more. It was transactional. Why? Because they hunted the same species as New England's commercial fishing fleet. Because they were viewed as competition.

It wasn't just the disappearance of the seals that led to the decline in the white shark population off New England. The sharks themselves were viewed as monsters—little understood, much feared. With no fishing regulations on any shark species in the western North Atlantic until the 1990s, the effects of a maligned reputation stoked by bounties, government-encouraged shark fishing, and the so-called *Jaws* effect took its toll on a species that lives to seventy years of age and doesn't reach sexual maturity for decades. White sharks became menacingly emblematic, and while they'd become rare by the 1980s, every sighting stoked emotions that often sent sportfishing boats steaming from New England ports in search of the behemoths. Many white sharks were harpooned while feeding on dead whales. The sharks appeared oblivious to the shark hunter, who stood only meters above the fish as it raised its massive head from the water to rend chunks of blubber from the whale's flank. *Jaws* author Peter Benchley, who'd become a staunch advocate for shark conservation, likened it to shooting fish in a barrel. Once harpooned, they fought the shark, exhausted it, and dragged it to the boat. Two Magnum loads of buckshot into the head. "That took the life out of him," a sportfishing captain said, as he lashed the animal to the side of his boat—a trail of blood streaming from the gaping wound into the boat's wake.

The heart of Maine rests within the Penobscot River watershed. Like a tree with its steadfast trunk planted nearly equidistant between the Piscataqua River at Kittery and the Lubec Channel Downeast, the watershed grows up toward Maine's crown and out to the borders with New Brunswick to the east and Quebec to the west. Its heartwood is Katahdin—the Great Mountain. Like free-running sap, the river is lifeblood. The river nourishes its soul revealed in the plants and animals that inhabit it. Bear, deer, and moose. Pine, spruce, and hemlock. We travel there—to Baxter State Park; to Katahdin Woods and Waters National Monument—and we see pristine beauty in the spring snow that clings to Katahdin's bulk. We see wildness in the crash of a moose through tussock sedge and bluejoint grass. We see the Penobscot River surging like a healthy adolescent through Exterminator Hole and Cribworks Rapid and then confidently wending through dense green forests with the sagacity of the ages. But as I sit beside the fire listening to the coyotes, I'm thinking more about what we don't see. Even here in Debsconeag Lakes Wilderness Area, home to thousands of acres of mature forests and the highest concentration of pristine, remote ponds in New England—even here there is loss and degradation. There is an absence— a void my imagination wants to fill by turning the persistence of the coyote into the prudence of the wolf.

Centuries before the U.S. Bureau of Sport Fisheries (the precursor to the National Oceanic and Atmospheric Administration) encouraged fishing for sharks and shark tournaments with cash prizes, the wolf was hunted from this landscape by hard men clinging to the edge of the continent. They were beleaguered by the wilderness and beholden to their beliefs, and instead of seeing, as Aldo Leopold did, the "fierce green fire" in the wolf's eyes, the colonists saw the eyes of the devil. They relentlessly cleared the land for their livestock and for moral superiority. They pushed back the dark woods that loomed in their psyche both for what it was through experience and what it represented in Sunday sermons. Called from their beds by the bleating of sheep on a moonless night, demonic eyes were envisioned in light refracted through the heavy glass of a farmer's lantern held aloft. There was a musket in the other hand. The first bounty on wolves in North America was among the very first statutes established by the colonists. In the 1620s in Plymouth, citizens were encouraged by a bounty to destroy "those ravenous creatures." By the 1630s and 1640s, the Massachusetts

Bay Colony likewise enacted bounties that made the slaughter of the wolf as both American and religiously motivated as John Winthrop's "City on a Hill" sermon.

The fire's coals are still hot, but the flame flickers less. I prod the coals with a stick, sending sparks like phosphorescence into the darkness of a sky opaque as a night sea. I think about what we've lost. I think about our connection to land and landscape. To wildness. I think about the eastern cougar and the wolverine. I think about the wolf. I think about how we changed the landscape through four centuries of hunting and farming. I think about how we viewed predators as competition for the hunter and a menace for the farmer. Unlike the peoples who lived here for millennia before we arrived, we did not view ourselves as like these animals—as a fellow apex predator. We did not admire their traits and their efficiencies. We did not see them as conspecifics in spirit even if not taxonomy. Instead, we saw ourselves as removed—existing outside of nature. We believed we could choose at will to enter or leave the wilderness, and to satiate something we still have trouble articulating, we created opportunities to simulate the experience of wildness without the risk. Patrolled and fenced parks. Documentaries. Virtual reality.

Perhaps incongruously within the immensity of the Penobscot River watershed on a dark night before a waning fire, I think again about the white shark returning to New England in numbers no living human being has ever seen. As the night cools and the water softly laps the beach, I feel the radiant heat of the coals on my face, and I think about what it means to restore an apex predator to an ecosystem. In 1972 the Marine Mammal Protection Act made it illegal to kill seals, and the seals returned. In 1997 the federal government made it illegal to kill white sharks, and the white shark population slowly recovered, thanks to the protection they were afforded and a growing supply of food. How can we not revel in the wonder of a conservation success story such as this?

But before the question finishes formulating in my brain, I'm answering myself like I'm no longer immersed in the beauty of this night. In much the same way that, upon reaching Penobscot Bay, those specific molecules of water cease to be what they once were at the headwaters, I'm overcome with the weight of history and our legacy. All that we have accumulated and built and believed. I know the effects of a fatality in the jaws of a white shark on Cape Cod in 2018 and another in Maine in 2020. I know how we react when challenged to consider once again what it means to be prey (even if only accidentally). There were calls for the culling of seals and the hunting of white sharks. Public safety officials and politicians were implored to implement mitigation measures to temper the wilderness with drones and detection systems able to alert lifeguards of a hidden danger lurking. America's carefree seaside playground should not be ceded, they said. It could not. Not now. Not after how far we have come and how technologically capable we are.

And yet the sharks are here, and in the intervening years between the fatalities and now, we are once again developing an uneasy truce with them. It is, however, a far different relationship from the one practiced by people who hunted from canoes alongside white sharks chasing the same prey thousands of years ago. Those who lived among wolves. Their relationship was forged in respect and interconnectedness, while ours is more transactional. We count our success by the number of ecotourists who are willing to pay to see a white shark in the wild or support white shark conservation with a financial gift that gives them the "right" to name the shark. We argue that we have made a living white shark more valuable than a dead one. We balance research dollars against papers published, questions answered, and the accumulation of data. It's not that these things don't have their place—they do, but we need to go deeper. We need to be able to imagine hearing the howl of the wolf along the banks of the Penobscot again, and we need to never lose our ability to consider Wildness with nothing more than wonder, awe, and respect. It's not too late, but we must be willing to seek some of the answers from the past. The beauty of water is that those molecules can be infinitely rejuvenated through an ageless cycle. As a science writer, I love data and numbers, and yet I know that what we need goes beyond what I can quantify. It goes to a place where a canid howls into the night and a river continues to provide access to a past we desperately need to encounter.

i ride with her in silk

LISA PANEPINTO

we bathe the land
in blooms
river beds get clean
like we ask
sheaths of blue
carry wind
bat wing
owl plume
spider web
maple bark
goldenrod remember
to say hello to
snake in the wood
talk soft to jays
puddles elderly
new life unfolding
in the plants
ride through farms
swim with trout
feel our heartbeats
soothe the root tips

Scripture

KARA DOUGLAS

You went alone, before first light
to where still water broke into motion.

I imagined you at dawn, casting
and recasting your line, moving like breath

taken and exhaled, taken again,
a fisherman's scripture held lightly with fluid wrists.

I wear a trail upon the dusty Earth
remembering, forgetting, remembering.

When my knuckles whiten in a tight grip,
I recall, you went alone, before first light.

Welcome to the Penobscot, Pajaro Jai / Enchanted Bird

PATRICIA SMITH RANZONI

For the Chocoe Indian crew of the Panamanian ketch Pajaro Jai, *August 4, 2004*

Today's rains honor you, we swear, 3,000 miles afar, drumming on all our skins
the same way the sun shows us we are all kin, however far from home forests
we ride the water and wind.

News of you reached us outback where we left our summer work to greet you.
Left our wood piles we can't afford to leave in the few weeks remaining
    before frost.
Left our gardens we can't afford to leave to save what can be saved before
    the freeze
due to arrive not long after you.

> *Wish you could see it! See these shores snow white!*
> *See what we of the north see of Earth's death again and again*
> *followed by each undeserved resurrection come spring.*

And Johnny has helped make this cake to bring to town to catch you before
you sail upriver where our Native neighbors and friends are waiting with
    ancient rites.

This bay is theirs. We, crumbs of their history.

Here—flour, oats, seasalt, gingerroot, blackstrap, a bit of fat. Cinnamon, clabber with soda, today's eggs Ed just brought in for it, just-picked wild fruit from the ledge. A little lemon. Old-fashioned downcast Maine (because sails go down over the horizon) blueberry gingerbread still hot from the oven to say *welcome*.

To say *thank you* for resting here, showing us the deep maps of your tattooed faces and limbs bared in trust and what we've lost. Stirring our currents with
    your tongues
and songs. We know foreign sounds from vessels joining our people's work
at the paper mill you slept near but can you see our ears straining for the spice
    of yours?
That the very trees of our river shores are this moment leaning to your wings,
dreaming you nestling here?

> *Take this—the best we have to give, to show you how life here tastes.*
> *And in this way we give praise for your presence and go with you,*
> *wishing to know what you would have us know before lifting off.*

A Penobscot Bay Love Letter

Brenda E. Smith

February 14th

My Dearest,

I have loved you for all seventy years of my life. You've enchanted me since the first time my baby pink toes splashed in your shallow foam, thrilled by the sudden, cold swirling around my ankles. The best days of my childhood were those spent in your shallows, frolicking in your chilly, buoyant brine. For a few hours each day, as your tide ebbed, you exposed your hidden treasures, luring me to explore your shallow, rocky nooks for starfish, urchins, and tiny sidestepping crabs.

Over time, I have grown accustomed to your ever-changing moods, knowing better than to expect any consistency or predictability in your presence. I love you as much when you are serene as when anger seethes from your depths, casting spray as your powerful swells crash onto the land that restrains your fury. Your spirit is free and impetuous, and I adore how different you dare to be from day to day. Your vastness has no equal except for the sky above you, but even then, your two elements, water and air, join in an everlasting caress.

Your moist, salty mist beckons me closer. I revel in your cool silkiness as you swallow me, wrapping my body in your embrace. I am delighted by the gentle rocking of your swells as I float up and over them on a steamy summer's day. Once, when I doubted your might, you knocked me off my feet and dragged me shoreward, as a mother rebuking her child for ignoring danger, warning and teaching at the same time.

When I feel sad or hurt, I seek comfort in you. Perched on a driftwood log, I can pour out my heart to you while you listen patiently. My deepest secrets I have confided to you, knowing you will hold them tight within your grasp. Your sweet lullaby soothes me as your waters melodically tickle granite beach stones worn smooth by eons of your persistent, sculpting touch. You never judge me; rather, at your side, I find serenity and the space to clear my head and weigh my options. You invite me to walk along your sandy shore and dare me to escape your playful surges reaching to soak my feet with your kisses.

Some days, when the sun reflects at just the right angle, your surface twinkles like diamonds with a billion specks of radiance that fill my heart with ecstasy. Your gifts have been far greater than I ever could have imagined. I want to memorize moonbeams from a full moon shimmering across your surface and recall the haunting late-night cry of a single loon aching for a soulmate as it drifts along your shoreline. I want to dance with your frothy whitecaps that curl and twirl with feisty abandon to nature's wind song.

For however much time I have left to live, I intend to stay by your side. I wish I could be with you forever, as certainly you will flourish until the end of time, while my tide is relentlessly receding. Your wild beauty is the last thing I want to see when my eyes close for the final time in this life. I love you, my dearest, beyond words.

With all my heart,

Your loving soulmate

if she remembers

Gabriella Fryer

we all went out
one horse at a time
until the dust settled
over our hair
and skins

we believed we turned
all the subtle colors
of the earth
forget-me-not blue
burnt orange
golden
then violet
dusk

and after the sun fell

we thought
we had become great
horned owls
bears
beavers
sly-pawed raccoons
but they don't understand
our talk

they only hear the black
of our footprints
the clang of our metal
bang

we left their rotting meat
in the river

and I wonder if she remembers
when I swim in her waters
when my children delight in her sounds

Into the Forest

MEADOW RUE MERRILL

Early Saturday morning, I meet Dustin and Emmy by the abandoned school bus. We'd found it in the woods earlier that summer while camping in Maine with our families. As soon as I step through the pines, Emmy's big black lab, Jack, wiggles all over like he's covered with fleas.

"He likes you." Emmy grins, holding onto Jack's collar as he nudges my hand with his nose.

"He's probably hoping I brought cookies," I say.

Dustin eyes my pack. "Did you?"

"Nope." I unzip my bag. "But I brought these!" I dig out three Tootsie Pops from the stash I'd bought while working for Mrs. Dunn at the camp store. Her husband "Mr. D" had grown up on an Aroostook potato farm, but he'd died the previous summer, leaving behind dozens of baskets that he'd woven by hand.

"My favorite!" Emmy picks red. "Why do you think I stop by the store so often?"

"To see me?"

"Because with braces I'm not allowed to eat candy." She peels off the wrapper and pops the lollipop into her mouth.

Dustin picks orange. Guess I was as wrong about him as he was about me, I think, remembering the morning I'd bought them. Dustin's dad is the camp handyman. Let's just say, we got off to a bad start. I'm just glad his dad convinced my parents that it was safe for us to hike to Great Lake. For the past few weeks, we've been searching for Mr. D's secret grove of brown ash trees—the ones he used to weave his baskets. Dustin says they are somewhere between the campground and the lake. We need to find them to make sure they are safe from the emerald ash borer, an invasive beetle that has been slowly killing all of the world's ash trees. Even though she's been extra protective lately, Mom agreed to let me go as long as I promised to stay with Dustin and Emmy and not to go in the water.

As we tramp along the edge of the riverbank, mosquitoes cover my bare arms and legs like mini tattoo artists. I slap them away, wishing I'd worn pants and long sleeves. The trees are so dense, the branches scratch my skin, leaving red marks. We walk single file. First Dustin, followed by Emmy, then me. Jack pushes ahead, splashing in the river.

"Gross!" Emmy spits, wiping at her face. "I think I just ate a spider."

"Does Maine have coyotes?" I ask, wondering what else might be out here.

"Plenty." Dustin holds back a stray branch so it doesn't swing back and hit Emmy. "But they don't bother people."

"What about bears?"

"Plenty of those, too. But black bears mostly eat plants, so you're safe, unless you're a blueberry."

I laugh nervously, but having Jack along makes me feel safer. Even if he is pretty goofy. The farther we go, the more I begin to relax. The quiet stillness of the woods slowly seeps inside me, making me feel quiet and still, too. The soft gurgle of the river reminds me of my grandma Gigi's ceramic jug, the one shaped like a trout. When Gigi poured iced tea from its mouth, it made a glugging sound, which always made my sister Mae laugh. If only she could hear this. But Mae could only go on walks with wide, smooth paths for her wheelchair. Nothing as rough as this.

"We should walk in the river with Jack," Emmy says, balancing on a log to avoid a dense patch of prickers. "It would be faster."

"Until you slip on a rock," Dustin says.

"I'd risk it to escape these horseflies." I swat at a fat green fly bombing my face.

"Why do you think I wear a hat?" Dustin swooshes it around his head.

While we walk, Emmy tells Dustin about Megalith Man, the new character her script-writer mom is creating for the next season of *Doom Fighters*. While her Mom works in LA for the summer, Emmy is camping with her grandparents. "Whenever he's in danger, he transforms into a rock."

"Don't move!" Dustin freezes, pointing at a moss-covered ledge. "That rock wasn't there a minute ago. Oh, no! It's moving! Run for your lives!" He crashes through the undergrowth as Jack scrambles after him.

"Fine." Emmy gives her black-and-gold braids an irritated shake as Dustin doubles over, laughing. "So, if you could invent a superhero, what would you be?"

"Anything?" Dustin asks, waiting for us to catch up.

"Anything." Emmy nods.

"That's easy," Dustin says. "Acorn Man. That way I could grow roots and stay right here. No more moving at the end of every summer when the campground closes and my dad has to find a new job. What about you?"

"Moon Woman!" Emmy touches her fingers together above her head and twirls through a patch of ferns. "So, I could look down and see everyone I love— like my mom—even if they're far away."

I remember the first time I'd seen it—the moon. Not in a picture book or out the window, pale as soap above the bright city lights. *Really* seen it. Late one summer night, walking on Long Sands beach in York with Dad. The path it blazed across the water shone so bright it looked like you could walk clear to the end of the world. How old had I been? Six? Seven? And where was Mae? Probably in our rental cottage with Mom because it took so long to get her ready for bed. It made me sad. Had Mae ever seen the moon?

"What about you, Cailyn?" Emmy turns to me. "What would you be?"

Last year, I might've said Soccer Girl, so I could outrun opponents and score the most goals in a game. But now? "God." It slips out before I even know it's there.

Dustin snorts like that's even funnier than Megalith Man. "God?"

"You know that's bad, right?" Emmy's eyes bug wide. "Grann says that's why everything down here's such a mess. Adam and Eve. Ever heard of them?"

"Of course, I've heard of them." I roll my eyes and keep walking. "My mom teaches Sunday school. At least, she used to."

"So, you know about the apple?"

"What apple?" Dustin asks.

"The one from the Garden." Emmy throws out her hands, like *What kind of an idiot are you anyway?* "When God made the first man and woman, he put them in a garden. It was perfect. No death. Nothing bad. They were allowed to eat from any tree they wanted, except one."

"Which one?"

"The Tree of the Knowledge of Good and Evil. Then a snake slithered up and said that if they ate from *that* tree, they'd be as smart as God. So, they did."

"A talking snake?" Dustin laughs. "And they fell for it?"

"Maybe it was the first snake they'd ever seen." Emmy shrugs, swatting a mosquito. "Or maybe it just looked like a snake. Anyway, as soon as they disobeyed God, *KAPOW!* He kicked them out of the Garden. Then everyone started getting sick and dying and stuff."

"Sounds like Yggdrasil," Dustin says.

"*Ygg*-what?" Emmy sounds like she's choking.

"The sacred tree at the center of the world," Dustin explains. "It's from a poem my dad used to recite to me when I was little: *An ash I know, Yggdrasil its name. With water white is the great tree wet.*"

"Wait." I duck under a tree limb. "There's an ash tree at the center of the world?"

"The Norse thought so," Dustin says and keeps walking. "This tree was so big its branches stretched all the way to heaven."

"I suppose it's possible," Emmy says. "My Grann says there's more we can't see in this world than what we can see, and she's seen an angel."

"For real?" I ask. In all my years of sitting in church, I've never met anyone who's claimed to see an angel. "What'd it look like?"

"Big." Emmy stretches up her hands. "When she was little, Grann was leaving Haiti with her family on a boat. They were in the middle of the sea when they got caught in a storm. Lightning flashed and waves washed over the sides of the boat. Grann was scared. Then she looked up and saw someone standing in the middle of the boat. He was taller than the mast. So tall she couldn't see his face. But he told her not to be afraid. When she looked again, he was gone, but she knew she'd be okay. And she was."

No wonder Emmy's Grann makes so many statues of angels. I wish I could see one. Then maybe I'd know that Mae is okay, the way Emmy's Grann knew she'd be okay in the boat.

"If there is a God, why would you want to be him anyway?" Dustin asks me.

So, I could've saved Mae. So, when she came limp and blue into the world, she would've turned pink and squalled like a hurricane and the nurse would've laughed and said that with lungs like that she would be an opera star instead of rushing her to the NICU, and Mae would still be here. But saying so feels fragile, like my heart is made of glass, and I don't want anyone to see what's inside. So, instead I say, "I just thought it would be cool."

"While we're wishing," Dustin says, unscrewing the top of his water bottle. "Did either of you bring something to drink besides water?"

"Not me," Emmy says.

I shake my head.

"Now don't you wish Cailyn was God?" Emmy asks. "All she'd have to do is speak and—*BAM!* Coke would gush out of the ground."

Dustin laughs. But I'm still thinking about Mae—lying alone under a plastic dome—and I wish I really was God. Then I could've changed everything.

***

By the time we reach the end of the river, we haven't found any sign of Mr. D's brown ash trees. Great Lake stretches before us as bright and beautiful as something from the beginning of the world. Dustin, Emmy, and I stand on the shore as small waves ripple against the rocks.

"I don't get it." Dustin turns, looking back toward the trees. "Pines. All pines. Not a single ash anywhere."

"We must've missed them," I agree.

"How?" Emmy asks.

"I wish I knew." Dustin flings a stone, skipping it off the water.

Jack chases after it, so Emmy throws him a stick. He hurdles into the water, only his head visible as he swims after it. I'm so hot from our hike, I'd like to jump in myself, but remember my promise to Mom. Plus, I didn't bring my bathing suit. Jack swims back, dropping the stick at Emmy's feet. Then he shakes off, spraying us with water, and Emmy throws the stick again.

While Jack swims, we stretch out on the sun-warmed rocks. A pair of dragonflies buzz by, transparent wings reflecting the light. The sun feels so good on my bare arms and legs, I close my eyes, letting it fill me. How long has it been since I felt like this? Like part of something good. I wish Mom could feel it. I imagine her splashing back to shore, arms open wide, a smile spread across her face.

"Either of you bring something to eat?" Dustin asks, breaking the spell.

Emmy reaches into her pack and pulls out a small plastic box. "Coconut candy," she says, peeling off the lid. "Grann makes them."

The candy is soft and sweet like saltwater taffy. "What's that?" I point at a group of trees that look like they are floating in the middle of the lake.

"Crow Island." Dustin takes a second piece of candy. "The crows from around here roost there in the winter. Years ago, some family had a camp out there, but a kid wandered down to the lake one summer and drowned, so no one much goes out there now."

The sweetness in my mouth suddenly turns sour, and I wish I hadn't asked. "We should start walking back." I stand up, checking my phone. Almost noon. "I don't want my parents to worry." Then I remember that I'd promised my little brother Abe that I'd take pictures, so I snap a few photos.

Emmy calls Jack, and we grab our packs, tracing our way back toward the river. As the shadows close in, I look for trees with even pairs of almond-shaped leaves and roots that reach up from the ground. No one talks, but it feels like we are all wondering the same thing.

How are we supposed to protect Mr. D's trees if we can't even find them?

The Poetic Edda: The Mythological Poems, trans. Henry Adams Bellows (New York: Penguin, 2004), 13.

Author's note: This story takes place at a fictional campground near Lincoln, Maine.

Once Again, the River Runs Wild

ROBERT KLOSE

Until recently, my home was snuggled neatly between two dams along the banks of the Penobscot River here in central Maine. The behavior of the river was therefore a function of the human forces controlling the dams: at times it was a raging torrent; at others, a quiet lake. During spring runoff, when the river was the recipient of melting snows, the lower dam was sometimes closed and the Penobscot would rise precipitously, lapping at my backyard as I stood at water's edge, wringing my hands. But if the powers that be opened the dam, the river would drop to the point where I could almost wade across it.

This uncertainty has ended. A few years back, in a miracle of civic and political cooperation, several agencies came together and agreed to remove the dams, returning the river to its native state. For the first time in a hundred years, the Penobscot is a free-flowing river, muscling its way to the sea under its own power.

When I first caught wind of the plan, I was unsure where my sentiments lay: With those promoting hydropower as a clean, inexpensive way to produce electricity? Or with others who believed that rivers knew what they were doing and should be left alone? Now that I have seen the results of the dams' removal, I am happy that nature is again able to take its course.

When the dams were breached, the river's level dropped and it narrowed, exposing banks that had been submerged for generations. It was a beachcomber's dream. In the old days, the Penobscot was a dump site for those living along its shores. The depositories for household refuse existed at intervals, indicating that neighborhoods seem to have agreed upon common places to throw their trash. As I roamed the banks, I discovered all sorts of "memorabilia"—an old Coke bottle, a porcelain baby food container, a clay marble, a cast-iron toy truck, an iron wagon wheel, the blade from a buzz saw—all evidence of the industry, domestic and commercial, that characterized the river for countless years.

But the biggest boon of the dams' removal was the effect on the riverscape itself. While the contraction of the channel initially revealed some unappealing sights—tires and shopping carts—nature has been busy seeding the new beaches with all sorts of sedges, grasses, and wildflowers, which has invited the return of shorebirds and other wildlife.

Last spring, as I stood behind my house and peered out over the Penobscot, I caught sight of flashes of silver at the surface of the water. I took a closer look and realized that these were fish—thousands of alewives—leaping skyward as they made their way upriver to spawn, now that there was nothing blocking them. My impression at that moment was that this was more than simple migration; it was exuberance.

And so, I now live along not merely a river, but a river renewed. The Penobscot had always been a wonderful and scenic—if unpredictable—resource for me; but now it's become a movable feast. The drop of the water's level, combined with its unimpeded course, has created a restless scene, with all sorts of interesting eddies and stretches of white water, and bald eagles perched for their share of the largess. As I regard this river, one of the most scenic in America, the thought that occurs to me is this: As it was, so it is again.

But the promise of the Penobscot unbound is not yet complete. Many years ago, the river boasted a thriving Atlantic salmon fishery, with the first fish of the season going to the president of the United States. The dams helped to put an end to that era. But now, with the dams gone, there is renewed hope that salmon, the crown jewel of the Penobscot, will find their way home again.

Queen of Pines

"TWINKLE" MARIE MANNING

I came upon her
in a clearing that was calling me.
I was standing at the door of the white wooden church,
when she began to whisper.
Even as the setting sunlight glistened through the trees, offering brief glimpses of
Chesuncook Lake, I began to pull the door shut behind me. I followed the gentle
beacon toward the water, then left toward the woods.

Feet trodding down a tiny, winding, yet well-worn path to the shore just beyond.
Toward the clearing. Toward her.
"I can feel them in my bones," I heard her whisper.
"I can feel them, and you, in mine," I whisper back.

I round the bend and there she is, arms outstretched high above her trunk. I can
see the echo of her once-gloried fullness, where bountiful branches adorned with
noble needles would have been.
Yet what remains has been struck by lightning, a year, perhaps two past. Her
graceful body now gray and black with mere glimmers of auburn hinting
through. Bark of many colors crumbling in piles on the ground surrounding her.

Did she hold her arms skyward awaiting—even requesting—perhaps daring, the
bright white adversary? Was her posture a stance of defense or acceptance?

She survived the King's mandated desecration of her kind.
Survived his lifespan, and then his kin's;
was touched by Thoreau and many seekers since.

Holy of holies. Shrine to the Goddess.
This, she who is at once one with all Nature, yet alone in her isolated realm.
She who sees and feels and knows.
Her roots run wide and deep.
They shall remain.
They shall remain.

To Be of the River

KATIE COPPENS

Ice, *of* the earth
slowly shifts
heavy glaciers
pause
advance
pause
advance
cutting, carving, changing
land that will one day
shape the rivers,
sources of springs,
snowmelt, and lakes
propelled onward,
downward
a choreographed dance
of descending
fresh water
to the salty sea.

Like meandering veins
run throughout,
carrying oxygen,
sustaining life,
rivers do the same,
all pieces
of something whole.

Over 5,000 miles of rivers
once unmeasured
in the once nameless land
now divided, fractured,
and labeled as Maine;
the longest river
now called Penobscot
named for the
Pɑnawɑ́hpskewi,
the people of
where the white rocks
extend out.

The people *of*—
their drums
echo honor,
reverberate respect,
beat in rhythm
with the land, water, sky.
The people *of*—
sing songs of
gratitude.

The people *from*—
take and take.
A new noise—
the march of machines and motors
grows louder.
The people *from*—
control and claim.

The drums continue,
alongside ancestral song
they also beat
calls for change.
The river *of*—
is polluted by power,

clogged by chemicals,
interrupted by dams—
water slowed, blocked, and diverted,
fish stopped on their journey home.
The food web severed—
We, too, can be
severed,
disconnected pieces
of something whole.
To be *of* the river
when water becomes sick,
we do, too.

The drums—
that some ignore,
or worse,
try to silence,
continue on,
beating, Beating, BEATING.
Finally, some listen
and allow themselves to hear.
Senses awaken.
Some perceive what
they did not see.
Some believe what
they did not feel.

We are all pieces
of something whole.
We are all *of* the river.
When rivers heal,
we do, too.

The Lost Child of Bangor's Waterfront

MICHELLE E. SHORES

The wind whipped around the corners of the buildings, blowing snow in circular patterns on the cobbled street. The overcast sky gave way to frequent snow squalls and gusty winds on this frigid winter's day. Across the street from the row of tenement houses that lined Bangor's waterfront lay the mighty Penobscot River, frozen and quiet. Temperatures had stood well below freezing for several months now. Ice hung from the eaves; snow lay deep over the barrels and boxes stacked on the docks; the silence of winter lay over everything.

The streets along the waterfront were empty. With the river closed until spring, the shipping houses were shuttered and devoid of any activity. Without the arrival of the ships, there were no laborers lurking around the docks trying to earn a living. Also absent were the sailors, suffering from long days at sea and looking for entertainment onshore. The lumbermen, the mainstay of the waterfront economy, were way up north in their logging camps until spring.

There was no money to be made on the waterfront this time of year. No money to earn meant no money to spend either. The taverns and grog shops, which catered to the much-sought-after vices of weary hardworking men, saw their business dwindle. Only a few remained open to serve those trying to stay warm. Men sat idle around the stoves in their threadbare coats, backs hunched over, staring mindlessly at the floor. They drank away the weight of their responsibilities, mostly on credit, looking forward to spring.

The tenement buildings that faced the Penobscot River stood as stark shadows against the winter sky. A tallow candle lit a window here or there, but what little light they gave off was hard to detect through the filth and grime that covered the panes of glass. The bare clapboards of these unpainted buildings had been weathered to a dull gray, and inside they were a maze of walls and doors.

Originally built for other purposes, such as warehouses, these buildings had been remodeled as the influx of immigrants put a strain on the community. There was no thought or plan to their design. Walls were put up and torn down depending on the need. A larger space created for the Irish family with nine children. A smaller section was partitioned off for the Hungarian man who lived alone and peddled tin. As tenants came and went, the layout of the building changed to accommodate the new arrivals.

There was no insulation against the cold from the outside or from the sound of your neighbors on the other side of the wall. The crying of children, the drunken arguments between husband and wife, and the sounds of others rollicking in ecstasy were heard by everyone in the building.

Each apartment contained only the basics for survival: a room or two, a small stove, maybe a window if you were one of the lucky ones. Water was available at the town well a few blocks away; a couple of wooden outhouses in the alley were shared by everyone.

Winter's snow covered the dirt and litter on the outside of the building, leaving a clean appearance that was in stark contrast to what was found inside. The hallways were dark, windowless areas. Stray cats lingered hoping for a handout or a warm place to sleep. Laundry hung from lines stretched the length of the hallways, making it necessary to duck under the shirts or pants of your neighbors to enter your own doorway. Discarded bottles, broken packing crates, and the odd shoe with a hole in the toe were strewn about as physical reminders of the despondent lives of most of the residents.

As winter took its hold on the waterfront, it seeped into this building with incredible force. Only twelve degrees outside, it was not much warmer than that in the apartment of James Sullivan. He had left Ireland a few years ago with nothing but the strength of his back and a determination to make a better life for himself. He had worked in the lumber camps around Mattamiscontis until an accident had laid open his left leg. He had nearly bled to death. Now, walking with a limp on a weakened leg, he couldn't find work in the camps any longer. He swept floors a couple days a week in a local shop. He earned enough to buy the rum he needed to survive, but not much else.

James had one small room to call his own in this tenement on Washington Street. In the center of his room stood the small coal stove with the pipe extending off toward the back wall. Black soot left a film on the wall where the pipe leaked smoke into the room. Cold air could be felt as it rushed in around the pipe; the hole having been cut haphazardly, it didn't fit properly. The stove too was cold; there hadn't been money enough to buy coal now for several days. A small wooden table sat in one corner, both of its accompanying chairs tipped over, evidence of an argument or a drunken stumble. The table itself was strewn with rum bottles, a wooden bowl that contained more mold than food, and a bucket of water that was frozen solid. In the opposite corner, lying on the floor, was a straw tick mattress; a small tear in the side allowed the mice to scavenge material to line their own nests within the walls. In another corner sat the chamber pot. The bitter cold kept him from venturing outside, so this pot was full to the rim and overflowing. The brown liquid frozen in a stream where it had run to the corner of the room via the slanted floor. The smell of human waste, body odor, rotten food, and stale alcohol hung heavy even in the cold air.

Lying on the mattress is seven-month-old Timothy, his body blue from the cold. He hasn't had anything to eat for a couple of days and the weakness, combined with the cold, has left him motionless. Too sick to even cry, he coughs occasionally, his eyes staring without blinking out into the room. He is wrapped in a man's old sweater, probably one that belonged to James, and his only other piece of clothing is a diaper. His diaper had been put on a few days ago, probably around the time he was last fed, and is now fully soiled. The areas of his diaper not in contact with his body heat are partially frozen.

Also in the room is Stephen's mother, Bridget. Hailing from County Cork in Ireland, Bridget had first arrived in St. Stephen, New Brunswick, where she made a few dollars selling herself to anyone coming off the arriving ships. Hearing of the wealth that could be made along Bangor's waterfront, she had found her way here, only to learn the work disappeared in the winter. There weren't enough men during the winter to provide a livable wage to all the women willing to share their beds. In addition, the birth of Timothy last summer had certainly added to her troubles. Short of stature, with flaming red hair that made apparent her Irish heritage, she had the temper and stubbornness to go with it. She also had a love of rum. As she lay now on the floor, she couldn't remember the last time she had eaten or when she had fed the boy. In fact, she didn't recall when she had first arrived in this room or how many days she had even been here. She drifted in and out of consciousness not really caring if she lived or died.

The neighbors were the first to notice that something wasn't right in James Sullivan's apartment. It was common to hear the arguments of everyone, but this one was getting louder and had been going on for some time. In adjacent rooms children stared down at their plates or buried their heads under their pillows as the flickering candles cast shadows on the walls that seemed to move with the commotion. Wives spoke in hushed tones with each other in the hall-ways and then reported back the latest gossip to their uninterested husbands. When Bridget had screamed, followed by the thud of her body striking the wall, that was enough for even the hardest of souls, and the city marshal was quickly summoned.

The stench that hit the city marshal when he opened the door to the unheated apartment only added to his shock at the conditions he found the room in. Both Bridget and James were naked, their bodies almost as blue as little Timothy who lay close to death on the bed. Their clothes were lying on the floor in scattered piles, indicating that they had begun this day in the trappings of passion, but it had gone wrong somewhere along the line. Both were heavily intoxicated, numbed not only by the cold but by the quantity of rum they had spent their meager earnings on. Bridget had two black eyes and blood seeping from what was obviously a broken nose. She lay in a fetal position on the floor near the over-flowing chamber pot. Her unwashed red hair fanned out among the feces and urine, her body bruised and dirty. She lay crying, squeezing herself tighter and tighter into a ball. James was pulled from his drunken stupor and set abruptly into one of the overturned chairs that had been righted by the city marshal. As he was questioned, his shoulders slumped and his head hung downward. All he could focus on was the long angry scar on his left leg. It was a testament to when things had started to spiral downward in his life. As another squall of snow began outside, no one even noticed who wrapped little Timothy in a blanket and hurried him off to the almshouse.

The room in the tenement building was quickly let out to someone else. The scant personal belongings of James and Bridget put out into the hallway to be claimed by anyone else in need. Winter held its grip on the waterfront for another three months. With the spring freshets came the logs and the lumbermen. The ice melted and the mighty Penobscot reopened, bringing in the ships laden with goods and men to revive the lagging economy. James Sullivan found work in a tavern filling drinks for thirsty men. Bridget was there, too, but quenching another kind of thirst of lumbermen and sailors who had not seen a woman in months. She never bothered again with her son, Timothy, who remained at the almshouse registered under the name of Timothy Sullivan, although James was not his father. Next to the child's name in the ledger book someone finally wrote "adopted after 238 days," indicating how long he had remained there.

Timothy's past was swept away like the melting snow in spring as there are no records of who adopted him, no way of knowing who he became, his future as unknown as his past. Timothy disappeared into history just as Bangor's working waterfront was being replaced by a cleaner and more sustainable waterway. In the winter the Penobscot still freezes, the wind still whips the snow, but now traffic flows over the spot at the intersection of Oak and Washington Streets, where the tenement building once stood and history reminds us of its link to our present.

Author's note: This is historical fiction based on an 1859 account published in the Bangor Whig & Courier *and additional research done by the author.*

Great Blue

Leslie Moore

The heron lifts off
its granite pedestal
with primordial
grandeur,
a pterodactyl
come back
to life.

Ponderous
but aloft,
it skims the bay
with giant
wingbeats,
head tucked,
neck coiled,
legs trailing.

I too want
to rise from
this rocky shore,
redeemed,
and flap into
the great blue
beyond.

Poetry Camp Duck Club

GARY RAINFORD

A badling of eighteen ducklings
and their watchful momma scratch
their way to my doorstep, peeping
and making soft, throaty, chucking sounds

like guzzling wind. "Hello, beautiful
babies," I say, scooching to the bottom
step. "And thank you, Momma,
for visiting." She swivels, like a turnstile,

waddles toward me, stops at my feet,
looks up, and stares blankly into my eyes.
"My drake," she says, *"abandoned us.*
His shimmering green head, his chestnut

chest, the blue speculum on his wings
bordered by thick, light-gray lines, the
black coverts with white outer tail feathers,
and his bright orange legs and feet

attract predators. He is dangerous."
Then her downy ducklings swing
around, all of them, lockstep like soldiers.
I can reach out and touch their poofy,

dandelion seedhead feathers, cuddle them
like kittens, but I don't want to disrupt this
blessing from Long Lake or startle Momma,
whose manner is as holy as motherhood.

The Blood Moon Returns

MEG WESTON

In early dark, the moon was full when I walked the dogs.
The clocks turned back this week, and we were adjusting
to new times. The searchlight in the sky interrupted
each step, interrogated the ragged outlines of my grief,
extended shadows across the road to bar my steps.

Planets hung low in the evening sky.
Just nigh a year since the moon last turned red,
when your blood froze in your veins.
It's hard to believe a year has passed ...
your son turned three without you.

A year ago, I lay awake at night after hearing
the news, I felt, but didn't watch, the eclipse.
But this year, by early morning I watched
a crescent of light fade into a pale
scream of red. I hung on to see a sliver
of your smile like the Cheshire cat in the trees,

until the moon fell into earth's shadow.
Until the eclipse stopped time, I walked among
moon-shadows, and traveled
through a forest of memory,
this lunar orb
watching over you,
over me.

Narrow River to the North

KATHLEEN ELLIS

Over 8,500 miles of rivers and streams in the watershed flowing, rising,
surging, draining, damming, clogging, icing, evaporating,
roiling, transporting, irrigating, silting, flushing,
absorbing, churning, pulsing, receding,
merging, rippling,
falling
heed
less
ly

Water Wisdom at Play

Sarah Carlson

Morning widens softly along the riverbank.
Sunbeams stream through rustling leaves
as I rekindle the campfire,
sit quietly as others awaken.
I'm drawn to the water's edge,
watch playful swirls and riffles as they slide on by.
I listen to the melodic rumble of upriver rapids
and sensations of yesterday's swim stir within.
Diving across the eddy line,
right where the rapid begins to settle.
Joining the rush,
savoring a giggle that surfaces
with the swiftness of the ride.
Watching the shoreline,
deciding when to use
a few powerful strokes to navigate
back across the line,
feel the upstream pull,
relax in the reverse flow,
return gently to where the swim began.
I sigh with delight at yet another
lesson from the wild.
There are times to plunge and surge
or allow the flow
or curl back into oneself to rest.
Water wisdom at play
once again.

The Dark Trout

Matt Bernier

I was tired of walking into coniferous forests
and thinking only of valleys of shadows,
so one day, in my age of enlightenment,
I hiked into Lily Pad Pond amidst the mists,
a pilgrim strolling a Buddhist path of paths,
exiting a towering cathedral of white spruce
as those wooden doors swung open to a
shoreline lined with the sullen, swirling spirits
of passed fly fishermen, lost disciples,
fog obscuring the far shore where
a bull moose baptized itself over and over,
and I launched a leaky, particolored canoe
into tea-colored water that reminded me of
lapsang souchong sipped beside a campfire
on an empyreumatic evening in Maine,
incense of wood smoke and pine resin
rising from a warm, bottomless mug,
and I couldn't see this pond bottom either,

stirring this tea with an unvarnished paddle
the breadth and color of a bull moose's antler
as I glided past water lilies, lotus blossoms,
and recalled how Siddhartha was a prince,
so I tied a Prince nymph onto my leader
and the copper bead, gold wire and peacock herl
sunk into the unclear and unknowable,
me casting again and again, meditatively,
until the other side of consciousness tugged,
and just before the sun inflamed the clouds
with the saffron colors of Tibetan monks' robes,
I landed a ten-inch-long native brook trout
so dark its bright spots were barely lit,
trout as tarnished as a copper tea set in
the tannic water, its all-seeing, all-knowing
eye peering at me in metaphysical challenge
until I quickly released the fish, knowing,
even then, it would never release me.

My Triangle

HANK GARFIELD

Draw an isosceles triangle with its apex in Old Town and its long sides running through Port Clyde and Prospect Harbor, and that's my *home*. It's the place I've always returned to. It's the place I'd take up arms to defend or go all Greenpeace on my little sailboat to preserve. It's where I'll make my stand as the years close in.

My triangle covers the lower Penobscot River and the bay of the same name. Like most white settlers, I discovered the bay, and the mighty river that feeds it, from the outside in. My earliest memories are of drives up Route 1 and childhood summers on Deer Isle, punctuated by the predawn rumblings of lobster boats. I learned to sail at about the same time I learned to walk. My family pulled up stakes in Pennsylvania and moved here for good the year I turned ten.

These days I keep a small sailboat in Rockland and live in Bangor, at the head of navigation on the Penobscot for boats with masts and keels. I always thought of Bangor as a winter place, for Christmas shopping at the downtown department stores before the mall went in, for orthodontist appointments, and very occasional air travel.

North of Bangor is the University of Maine, where I work, and Indian Island, and the watery woods that inspire much of the region's music, art, and culture. North of that, there be dragons. (I *have* been up north, but part of me still likes to think that the edge of the world lies about ten miles north of Old Town.)

The Indigenous peoples spent winters inland and summers on the shore, which seems like a lifestyle well-suited to Maine, now and in the centuries before colonization and tourism. The river was the avenue to the islands and the sea. To travel downriver was to leave home and travel to the edge of the world.

The perspective of my European forebears was exactly opposite. They knew what lay across the ocean. They had come from there. Mystery and the unknown were upstream, in a North American heart of darkness.

There were no bridges then. You could not stand in Bangor and look downstream and decide which riverbank to explore in your car, whether to follow the western shore of the bay to Rockland or the eastern shore to Stonington, two towns only twenty miles apart by water but inhabiting different twenty-first-century worlds. Both are farther from Bangor than they are from each other. To drive around the bay is a trip of eighty-six miles. The car culture sits uneasily on a triangle that is mostly water.

The real roads are liquid, and always in motion. Big schooners once waited at Fort Point for a fair wind and a rising tide to carry them upriver to Bangor. Logs floated downstream (and suffocated the river) on their way to the mills. Yet today the Penobscot watershed stands as one of the great American environmental success stories. The birds are back: bald eagles in Bangor and puffins on Egg Rock. The Penobscot Bay and River system is big, bold, and beautiful enough to encompass millennia of human history and a myriad of modern interests, from shipping to science to fisheries to tourism, to people like me, mucking around in small boats for the simple love of the place.

Following Neil

CLAIRE ACKROYD

The trophies are mostly gone. Two wooden canoe-shaped awards survive, memorializing triumphs on the Kenduskeag and Mattawamkeag Rivers four decades ago, but the incongruous faux-bronze Greek athletes were assigned to the trash years ago, their tiny marble bases repurposed as paperweights or miniature walls in my granddaughter's toy garden. One other memory survives—that of learning to run tricky white water in a racing canoe by following Neil Phillips down through rips and rapids, hoping, as we went, to learn to maneuver a boat with the effortless skill that he possessed.

Neil Phillips needs no introduction from me to anyone who has paddled the rivers and lakes of Maine. I knew of his life as a canoe adventurer, mentor to Indian Island kids, with whom he built and paddled war canoes, and as a driving force in the world of white water canoe racing. But mostly he was the safe path to follow down difficult water, and the interesting man who lived on an old bridge abutment on Orson Island, his home reachable only by canoe until the river froze over.

It was the simplicity and economy of his skills that we strove to emulate. Without seeming to break a sweat, he was able to beat the best of the nation's racers. Skill over strength, we said. Paddle well, not hard. Don't throw splashy whirlpools of wasted energy. Keep it smooth. Watch the water. Anticipate. Avoid extravagant corrections. Winning a race seemed incidental to the pleasure of developing some level of expertise—learning how to navigate white water as deftly as he did. It became our go-to survival plan. When in doubt, follow Neil.

Had it not been for these experiences, I might never have come to know and revere the river that we live alongside, and to understand its significance to the people who share its name. Neil has gone, and we will all follow him eventually, but the impact of one thoughtful, quiet, skillful man lives on.

The Mighty Penobscot River

PAM DIXON OERTEL

Turbulent
High water
Ever flowing

Miles and miles long
Industrial
Great
History making
Twisty
Years of prosperity

Penobscot Nation
Eons old
Noble
Opportunity
Boating
Salmon producing
Calming
One of a kind
Tree lined

Rocky shore
Icy
Vital
Energetic
Relevant

The Penobscot, Outside My Window

RHEA CÔTÉ ROBBINS

41 Years
By the riverbank
                The river in view
        the man sowed the
                        garden seeds
        to produce powerful
                vegetables
        for his children
to grow strong
        lean
                free.

        Snow falls.
They all slide down
        to the
                bottom
                of the hill.

                                (River like the
                        water road
                                of
                                other days
                                in view)

        river visible from

Dr. Wheeler's House
     on the Son-of-a-bitch hill
     the truckers call the
          incline in
          winter.
    Spring blossoms on apple
         trees, some ancient
             crab apples
         inspires art work
         series drawings of "medlars and sorb apples."

Summer. River hidden by the
         trees—water glistens between
            the blowing winds.
Passing time in oranges
     reds, browns
     leaves fall
     to expose the
     goodnights I see the
     river season again.
Winter follows—
the
flow never stops.

Bass and Black Glass

K.W. BERNARD

The slam of my car door echoed like a gunshot in the early morning stillness. I skidded down the embankment with my two-piece rod rattling between my fingers. The loose gravel delivered me beneath the enormous white pine that marked my favorite spot on the Penobscot. I high-stepped the poison ivy, drawn through the low-hanging hemlock boughs to the steady grumble and white glow of misty waters. Emerging from the clash of disturbed roadside and Maine woods, I trod on an outcrop that spent most months underwater.

From my position, the river ran unmarred by houses, and the forest cloaked the roads that hugged both sides. I scanned the banks, basking in the serenity that flowed with the water. Upstream and across from me, a new sun hung just above the tree line, wrestling with the fog to the north. Downstream, a deep pool stretched like black glass across a little cove. A small, straight log that hadn't been there last week protruded diagonally at its opening. Far beyond the cove's point, boulders weathered the river's wrath in wreaths of white water. Ahead, riffles and eddies danced with the sun's muted light on either side of a narrow channel.

That was my favorite part—the light split into glittering shards. If heaven existed, surely it hid in the sparkles where sunshine met water.

The roar of a big truck barreling down Route 2 cracked the tranquility. I was alone with nature but far from the wild.

After assembling my pole, I dug a nightcrawler out of the container. My insides squirmed with the worm as I pierced it with the hook. Excitement quashed guilt when I opened the bail for the first cast. I felt the tug of a hit within seconds of my bait striking the water, and I reeled against the pull of a fighting fish. My heart leaped with the joys of childhood as the bass erupted from the placid waters.

Swinging the fish close to my boots, I grabbed the line, then the bass. I'd caught my quarry, a smallmouth with gleaming, olive-bronze scales and intricate vertical markings. Long but lean. Nothing to brag about. I sent it home without a photo and picked a new worm for sacrifice.

Each cast yielded a fresh bass until I got hung up on downed debris concealed in one of the eddies. Adjusting my angle and slackening the line failed to free my hook, so I tightened the drag and reeled until the monofilament snapped. After tying on a new swivel, I hooked up a jitterbug.

In search of larger prey, I headed downstream along the cove. Stepping on the bases of the grasses and sedges, I tamped them down rather than wade through. Their saw-toothed blades weren't welcome to caress my hips now that so many bore ticks.

I cast toward the odd, tilted branch that had drifted from the cove's edge nearer its center. I let my lure float for a few seconds, drawing in only the slack, before reeling slowly with my rod tip up. The jitterbug wobbled through the water, gurgling as intended.

A few seconds after the lure vanished with a sharp tug, a bass jumped in a spray of glimmering droplets and a jangle of steel. It wasn't much bigger than my earlier fish, and I regretted the tangle of trebles as soon as I plucked it from the water.

Sandpaper teeth scratched my thumb pad as I worked at the hooks with needle-nose pliers. I sighed to ease the knitting in my chest and reminded myself that bass were bad for the native fish. They didn't belong there.

Of course, neither did I.

The fish shook, and I fumbled it, letting one hook catch the side of my thumb. Not so deep as to embed the barb, but enough for blood to bead on the surface. The crimson drop fell as I adjusted my grip, adding to the water without a sound. The tiny red plume hung just below the surface, a little trail of me, then became the river.

I freed the fish from the jumble of barbs and released my grip after swishing it into the pool to get water moving through its gills. It zipped away after one thrash, loosening the knot in my gut.

A heavy plunk yanked my attention to the deepest part of the pool, where thick ripples expanded across black glass. I eyed the massive log jutting into the calm, dark middle. Barkless and damp with morning mist, the once-lofty tree appeared slick. I wouldn't have thought twice about traversing it in my sneakers. But my agility suffered in knee-high muck boots, and I didn't trust the river. Too many people died in it. And I couldn't tell when it wasn't in the mood for me.

What were the currents doing beneath the motionless, obsidian surface of the cove? I stared at that peculiar, straight stick that had floated nearer the pool's center. How could it move upstream?

Still, I'd had enough treble hooks and small fish. I traded the jitterbug for my Plummer's frog. Whether the lure had come from my dad or grandfather, I didn't remember. But I knew I couldn't cast the irreplaceable treasure around overhanging branches.

I hopped on the log and gave every step the attention it deserved until I reached the farthest, steady perch. After smiling at the silly rubber frog like it was an old friend, I sent it flying into the cove's core. I aimed for the strangely cylindrical branch, where a jagged snarl of sunken limbs lingered, just visible beneath the surface. My frog hopped back to me alone.

A few fruitless attempts later, I lobbed my lure upstream into the blinding sunlight. No luck there, either. I decided on one last cast and turned back downstream. The weird limb had drifted even closer. As I worked my frog, I wondered if someone else's line had bound the downed wood to a giant fish or snapping turtle. Half vertical and not bobbing, the branch didn't seem like it should be able to float as it did.

The reel sang, stealing my attention, followed by my line. I tightened the drag and fought back, cranking furiously as the fish changed directions and headed toward me. My heart soared with the bass as it exploded from the water. I grinned—this one was big.

We battled for a minute before the bass rose from the black beside the log. As I reached for the fish, the inky water birthed a face behind it. Adrenaline cut through my thighs, and I froze. Huge, multifaceted eyes stared into mine from the alien visage beneath my reflection. My heart pumped molasses.

It had to be an illusion. But as I gazed hard into the blackness for an explanation, the sun perfectly highlighted what had half risen from the pool against the dark bottom. A triangular insectoid head hovered below, attached to a long, slender body that faded into the depths, but for its apex—that bizarre branch, poking above the surface like a snorkel. The aberration resembled a water scorpion only a million times bigger, and its visible limbs bore harsher ridges and spikes than any bug I'd seen. The raptorial forelegs were the same, though. And those extra-long appendages, studded with razor-sharp spines and tipped with chitinous scythes, were angled right at me.

In my mind's eye, I already hung impaled on those forelimbs, drowning with the leviathan's stout proboscis embedded in my abdomen, sucking out the blood and guts.

As still as the thing beneath the surface, I let the line slip from my fingers. The rod descended next, beside the creature, trailing after the fish. Seconds dragged like hours before I shed the paralysis. I sunk, slow and smooth, flattening myself onto the log. No sudden movements. With most of the aquatic horror's face consumed by its bulbous, blank eyes, the animate mass of thorns and branches had to be a visual predator.

Hugging the log, I inched backward. The monstrous mimic might have trouble snatching me from my perch if it had to peel me free. My breath caught with every shaky shimmy toward shore, and my nails dug so hard into the damp wood my fingers ached. Caught in the abomination's empty, black stare, I prayed with every push that my subdued undulations didn't trigger its prey drive.

When my feet at last floundered in empty air, the winch in my chest let go. Shoving myself up and back, I pivoted before both boots hit stony gravel.

I sprinted straight for the woods and scrambled up the embankment. I'd escaped. That nightmarish creature still lurked in the stygian pool, even if I didn't dare look over my shoulder to confirm it. But however hard I dug my toes into needle-coated humus and tore at the branches ahead, I couldn't get up the rise. Every panicked step revealed more hill and murky woods—ancient, old growth.

I paused as a dark shape coalesced ahead. A bear? Now that the sun had fled, I struggled to discern what moved toward me in the dim light. But the approaching figure floated down the hill, too tall and graceful for a black bear. Finally, as my brain caught up to my eyes, I recognized the shape as a man, broad-shouldered and square-jawed. He wore a shimmering black robe with a hood drawn over his head. Ridiculous. Maybe I was dreaming. Trapped in the most vivid nightmare of my life.

"What is—" My question died in my throat. Two voids of swirling ink where eyes belonged stared into me, at everything that I was. Ice water poured into my veins.

I spun and vaulted down the hillside, the danger in the river forgotten. The aquatic monstrosity just wanted my fluids. That thing with black holes for eyes … if it didn't eat souls, nothing did.

My heart thrashed against my ribs, and I struggled to keep my legs under me as I hurtled down the hill. Towering shadows closed in from the sides, slipping between trees in the margins of my vision. Somehow, I burst from the woods without wiping out.

The river didn't shine for me this time, not even with muted silver shards. Charcoaled clouds wouldn't allow it. I skidded to a stop just short of the water, half expecting to find the evil insectoid waiting to ambush me in the shallows.

But no shallows remained—or black pools. The river's depths were infinite and crystalline, populated by endless ebony tentacles. I teetered at the edge of the abyss, standing just inches above the water but with hundreds of miles to plummet. The midnight tendrils swirled and beckoned, tugging on my insides with whispers I couldn't decipher.

Maybe I'd already drowned. Fallen and hit my head when I stepped out on that log. Or might I be in a coma somewhere? Had I even woken up that morning? If I wasn't dead yet, I would be soon.

My muscles tightened, and my eyes burned at all the tomorrows snatched away. Those moments, promised to no one, that I felt entitled to—taken. Graduations, weddings, grandchildren, retirement. Stolen.

A pale hand fell on my shoulder, reminding me I had more to lose. Long fingers that terminated in black claws bit into my muscle. Ink wept from the nail beds, staining my shirt and numbing the skin beneath.

I prayed to every god of light who would listen for aid.

A low, ethereal laugh slithered into my ear on cold breath.

The Mystery of "Bagaduse" and the Penobscot Watershed's Monsters

LOREN COLEMAN

The Penobscot River and Penobscot Bay in central Maine contain mysteries aplenty. Within the field of cryptozoology, the study of unknown and as-yet-unverified animals, the Penobscot watershed may house creatures new to science and certainly of interest to zoological folklore.

As recently as early May 2017, a fellow named Alain Ducas was shooting video from the roof of the Hollywood Casino Hotel on Main Street, Bangor, Maine. Overlooking the Penobscot River, he captured some remarkable footage of a small humped creature, a so-called cryptid or river monster, floating by, with an extended neck sticking out of the water. Because he had an actual video, he shared it on social media, and the story quickly turned up nationally in the Boing Boing feed and via *Coast to Coast AM*. While the beast was never identified and the mystery remains, it was the talk of the town for some time.

After examining the footage, I found it almost identical to the Lake Champlain Monster, a subject I had written about extensively six years earlier. This footage was shown on the Eric Olsen "Champ" video from June 2009, filmed near Burlington, Vermont.

Station WPTZ said of the Vermont footage: "The video features almost two minutes of what appears to be a brontosaurus-like sea monster loafing off the shores of Oakledge Park near Burlington."

WCAX said: "A biologist at UVM thinks it may have just been a moose in distress. Another scientist says the video does appear to be legitimate."

The Penobscot River and the connecting bay have a long history of such enigmas going back to the Revolutionary War.

In Bernard Heuvelmans's classic cryptozoological text *In the Wake of the Sea Serpent*, he revealed a minor mystery to keen readers. Specifically, on pages 114, 144, and 575 of the 1968 English edition, he briefly mentioned a sea serpent sighting by British troops at "Bagaduse" in 1782.

Heuvelmans credited the story to the Reverend Abraham Cunningham, who related an account of the "British on their expedition to Bagaduse" having seen a "Sea Serpent" reportedly "300 feet long." Heuvelmans considered that size exaggerated, as it stood out as extreme during a time when most sea serpents sighted off the coasts of New England and Northeast America were said to be forty to sixty feet long.

Heuvelmans never found the location of Bagaduse, and he suggested in his book that it might be a misspelling of "Bogalusa"—a landlocked town in Louisiana that became infamous for its Ku Klux Klan activity.

In January 2006 the now-late cryptozoological author Michael Newton contacted me. He mentioned the Bagaduse mystery and asked for assistance. We exchanged emails. In one, Mike wrote: "Long story short, while reading Robert Heinl's *Soldiers of the Sea*—a history of the U.S. Marine Corps—I stumbled on a reference (p. 9) to a skirmish between jarheads [Marines] and redcoats [British] at Bagaduse Heights in July 1779. Apparently it's in Maine, at or near the site of present-day Castine, on or near Penobscot Bay. This fits perfectly with the time frame of Bernard Heuvelmans's report and also with the rash of eighteenth-century New England sea serpent sightings."

As fate would have it, living in Maine, I was one day away from traveling "Downeast" to the Castine area. I decided to do some field and local investigations of this Bagaduse mystery.

The locals quickly put me on the right track. It was "Bagaduce," not "Bagaduse." And they felt someone "from away" would have made such a "wicked silly" mistake, I was told in a pleasant Downeast accent.

So, it appears Heuvelmans had merely repeated an old spelling of the area or, more likely, a misspelling of the location in a retelling of the British "adventure" in Maine. Today, throughout the region you hear of the "Bagaduce" (not "Bagaduse").

The Bagaduce River flows through the small town of Penobscot and empties into the Penobscot Bay at Castine Harbor, about twenty-five miles northeast of Rockland. The locals view the Bagaduce River as an extraordinary body of water that graces the shores of Castine, Penobscot, and Brooksville, well known for its local wildlife. Today, traffic on the river consists of recreational craft, fishing boats, and training vessels of the Maine Maritime Academy in Castine.

The Bagaduce River is in Maine today, but technically, in 1782, it was part of the Commonwealth of Massachusetts. So during the battle at Bagaduce in 1779, the area was in Massachusetts. Perhaps this, too, has confused those seeking Heuvelmans's mysterious Bagaduse.

Maine did not become a state until 1820, when it joined the United States of America as the twenty-third state. Before then, it was known as the District of Maine and was an extension of Massachusetts.

Heuvelmans gave a hint that the Bagaduse sighting belongs in Maine. If you examine his "Chronological Table of Sightings" beginning on page 575, Penobscot Bay dominates the list around 1782.

Sea serpents were sighted in Penobscot Bay and near Maine in 1751, 1773, 1779, 1780, 1787, 1793, 1794, 1799, 1811, 1817, and 1818. Intriguingly, the vast number of sightings moved from the less populated areas of Downeast Maine to the more densely peopled locations of Portland, Maine, and Gloucester, Massachusetts, especially between 1817 and 1818. Before 1817, Penobscot Bay, Maine, was the number-one East Coast location for sea serpent sightings.

Portland's Cassie (Casco Bay sea serpent), as mentioned in *The Field Guide of Lake Monsters, Sea Serpents, and Other Mystery Denizens of the Deep* by Loren Coleman and Patrick Huyghe (Tarcher, 2006), may have become more well known in Maine. Still, the Penobscot Bay and the Bagaduce beasts were more frequent visitors to the District of Maine.

The Heuvelmans mystery of "where is Bagaduse" can be filed away now. It took place in the District of Maine, when it was part of the Commonwealth of Massachusetts.

Pines Stand

LEE SANDS

Pines stand
> Majestic

Lean sentries
> Keepers of centuries

Reflected
Clear and umber in
Penobscot waters

See Child—
> The Dawnland
> Sunrise

*

Closed eyes
> Still—

Hear
Chickadee trill and
> The cool
Lapping of the riverbank

Coaxing you
> First toes

> *

> *

*

Plunge

Into
The salmon run

        See them—

Swim Spurt
Swirl Sun

Where dreams spawn

*

Tail
Harbor seal
      Hungrily
Upriver toward
Brackish breakfast

Blubber-grin
      Whip
          Gnash

Surface

      Crash

Among
Crystalline bubbles
      and feathers floating—
Merganser, heron, osprey,

Eagle against the sun

See child—
      The eagle's wings
Reflected as your own

Soar
The watercourse
      Granite banked

> Tree-topped
Home

See the river—
> Water courses through you

Arteries
> Tributaries

Your
Silver-scaled lifeblood
> Gleams

East and West branches
> Gathering
North to south
> Gushing
Wide mouth gulf
> Gulping shellfish
Brine and whole tides

Fly child
> On high

Fly the
> Wild sky river

What
Bright reflections
Light your eyes?

Our future
> Heritage
> > Golden
Against the Dawnland sky

See it—
> (we see you)
> > Shine

No Salmon Were Harmed in the Making of This Poem

KATHLEEN ELLIS

For years we've eaten Atlantic salmon
once a week like clockwork, sometimes
Alaskan, but always American.

There's something patriotic in the act
of indulging in what's close to home, but
we've never eaten them from the Penobscot.

Endangered, yet we admire their resilience.
With their lateral lines, they've invented a way
to sense change in the magnetic field

and pinpoint the river they once lived in.
Last year over eight hundred were back,
not enough for a broodstock.
But don't think this is an elegy.
I've seen insects come back to life
after lying comatose for half a day.

I've seen a brook trout writhing in a pail
suddenly leap back into the river.
Wilderness enters our lives and we find

a way to greet it. Walking beside the river
past old logging booms, the rotting booms,
we hear the salmon navigating, slapping the water

like oars. We cheer them on as they pass by.
Count me in, they say. *Count me among the living.*

Follow the Stream

JOSH KAUPPILA

slight shuffle beneath
flowing feet. avoiding
brush, solidly placed.
scuffle of leaf pattern
ahead indicates animal
movement. direction
of tracks pull the imagination
between breaths, the foot falls
the body crouches.
the body stops, to soak
in sound and light.
all immediate questions
answered with awareness
a few breaths of calm,
ready the body to move again.
follow the stream: find coyote prints
follow deer and coyote prints.

through three bends of the river
do they overlap. and after the third
the coyote walks away
the deer tracks have gone.
crouching I see the drama,
see the paths to run and the
places to hide.
i think of the coyote eating the frogs
in the sandy shallows. the frogs which eat
the deep wood blackflies and mosquitoes.
i am just constructing a story.
dictated by the sun and the silence,
and the soil. how many stories
can we manifest, by being still
and following instinct?
where have our paths gone?

How to Catch a Salmon

CATHERINE SCHMITT

1. Spear it.

Over thousands and thousands of years, the Penobscot people developed many ways of catching fish: basket traps and sieve-like weirs, baited lines and bare hands. For *skamek*, the big, pink-fleshed, silver-scaled leapers that came from the ocean and migrated up the river each spring and summer, a long-handled, three-tined spear was the method of choice. Salmon—abundant, nutritious—were easy to spear where waterfalls and rapids slowed and concentrated their passage.

2. Net it.

Hundreds of years ago, newcomers to the river recognized Atlantic salmon from their homeland, knew how to catch the "King of Fish" in the Thames and the Tay, and they eagerly sought the familiar fish. But it wasn't enough to feed a family. They wanted more, and soon they were extending their fences out into tidal waters, funneling salmon into maze-like weirs with nets at their heart-shaped centers. The fish became a brand, and "Penobscot Salmon" soon fed many families, from the new state called Maine to colonies up and down the Atlantic shore. But the netters took too much, and took other things, too—trees and title, current and power—and soon they were netting fewer salmon than their fathers had before them. Some blamed the dams, but more blamed the "poachers." They banned the spear as they pushed the Penobscots out of their spearing grounds, all the while netting, netting, netting.

3. Lure it.

By 1900 the fly-fishing fad had found its way to the Penobscot Valley. Between the netters in the bay and the natives above the falls, the anglers snapped and waved their bamboo rods, conjuring salmon to the surface, tempting the fish away from their true goal, which was to make it over the dams and up through the rapids to the cooler, gravel-bottomed headwaters, there to wait for spawning season. Such was the skill and thrill of the sport, and the culture of fly-fishing inspired a new tradition, of sending the first sea-run Atlantic salmon caught in the Penobscot River to the president of the United States. This rite of spring continued from 1912 until the 1960s, when the netting, the damming, and the loading of the river with pollution became all together too much for the salmon to surmount.

4. Trap it.

For a while, the only people catching salmon in the Penobscot River were scientists working for the federal hatchery, who squeezed eggs and milt from fish trapped in the river and bred new generations. For decades, as other scientists and anglers and the Penobscot people fought to clean up the river, to block proposals for new dams, to tear old dams out, the biologists and hatchery workers kept the species alive, preserving enough genetic memory for the fish to maintain at least a few fragments of their wild character. The fish returned and the anglers renewed their traditions although more of them released their catch. But it wasn't enough.

5. Avoid it.

Too many dams still stood; legacies of pollution persisted; changes in Earth's climate rippled through the salmon's ocean food web. Maine had become the southern edge of the salmon's cold-water range, the Penobscot River home to the largest remaining run of wild Atlantic salmon in the United States. Scientists determined the precarious state of the population warranted endangered status. For all of the current century, it has been illegal to catch a sea-run salmon in the Penobscot River.

6. Imagine it.

The salmon are still here, however. In 2023 more than a thousand fish found their way from the Labrador Sea to the falls below Indian Island, where the *Panawáhpskewi people wait and watch and work to remove dams and clean up the river.* It was the largest run in over a decade. There are other fish here, too: alewives and blueback herring, sea lamprey and eels, sturgeon, brook trout, and rainbow smelt. Anglers have come back to the river, waving their wands for stripers and shad. To once again catch salmon in the Penobscot River requires two things: remembering the reality of it, and imagining the possibility.

From the West

MICHELLE CHOINIERE

From the West, it hurries,
    Over rocks and through the trees.
        Slicing through the heart,
            Flowing freely to the seas.
            Its history stretches,
                Carved along its twisting edges.
            The past: a tool,
          The star of many local legends.
        The present: a sanctuary,
Open wide and friendly.
        Forever it will run,
            Through the hearts of many.

Letting Go: Down by the River

Annaliese Jakimides

A cluster flock of pigeons tips across the sky,
      one breaking off to head somewhere
      none of the others is going

*

Soundtrack of my days and nights: Jamiroquai … Snoop Dogg … Handel … Carole King … A Tribe Called Quest … Debussy … Gil Scott-Heron … Nina Simone. I select each one individually, put it in the player, one at a time. Not every one. Not every day.

These days the order is shifting, but there is always somewhere in the mix my son's Jamiroquai, a group I never listened to until after he was gone. He'd given me three of their CDs at Christmas—his last Christmas. He gave them to me with no cases, no sleeves, no envelopes even. Just naked, exposed, vulnerable CDs balanced in the palm of his beautiful hand. Jamiroquai's "Feel So Good" is the first thing I danced to after the night he left us. There was no dancing for months—months and months—but when I finally danced, I danced to "Feel So Good."

It's playing this morning, and I'm dancing. Today is the day. It's already November. I've been procrastinating for weeks, and now very little time remains before the ice begins to crust over the waters of the Penobscot River that runs through the middle of my little city. This Penobscot is calm and controlled, so unlike the one I left a few years ago, the one whose confluences and tributaries and streams, the wildness, its dark brilliance, fed and circled and foundationed my son's life, our lives, millennia of lives, up north on the edges of the North Maine Woods.

A ceaseless, flowing movement—like music—constantly evolving, carrying us and our stories, our cultures.

Years ago, this river-on-its-journey used to carry logs from the north, where my boy learned everything, to this city, where they became nine-million board feet of lumber that then moved out into the world. Nine-million board feet over fifty years—just twenty-nine more than my son lived. I can't imagine how these shores with the Sea Dog restaurant, a few benches, and a parking lot could have sometimes held 3,000 ships at anchor.

In different stages and times, conditions, we adapt who we are to make the journey—be we river or human—and if we don't, maybe can't, there can be rupture, destruction.

Steady river for an unsteady son.

Here, now, some early mornings, sunlight shimmies through river crystals, a sure sign of impending winter. I've been on reconnaissance for days now, walking down by the riverbank, scouting out the best place. Requirements: light-filled, accessible, and definitely hidden from passers-by.

All of that seems an oxymoron of possibility, added to, of course, the need for this mother not to pitch and slip, slide down an embankment, scraped and damaged, losing her son, again.

For over a year I kept my son in the living room in the blue cardboard box I picked him up in. Sealed. Never opened. I was unable to consider my child as bone fragments. Months ago, when I decided he couldn't live with me forever, I moved him to the storage room in my apartment building. And there he's waited.

I know there are people who would ask me, why now? But the truth is that no one has asked where he is, whether I'm holding on to him, whether I've already let him go. I can't even yet explain to myself how I know the time is right. But I've known it for weeks now.

This morning breaks clean and brittle, a patina of sky through my bedroom window, crow flight in the foreground, crackles of newness as the city begins its citiness. Coffee, oatmeal. Check my email. Dance around my apartment. It's a normal beginning to an abnormal day. And now here I stand on the edge of my eight-by-ten storage room.

I have come for my son.

Yesterday I sorted through the green garbage bag of clothes the funeral home gave me months ago when I picked up the box of his ashes. I had held onto the socks, stiff and dirty like he always wore them, the sweatshirt his sister had given him that Christmas sliced down the back for its easy removal, the camouflage pants with his name printed on them, a small pack still carrying the paperwork for his instant tax return at H&R Block—the return that bought the gun. This morning only his pants are left—and the box—and him. Well, not exactly him. I know that. He can't be in a cardboard box, and *he* can't really be ashes.

The river isn't far from my apartment. I walk, my boy in a Shaw's supermarket bag. The handle breaks and he drops onto the sidewalk, still in his plastic bag that has popped out of the blue box I had slit open for ease of handling. I laugh as I pick him up, put him back in the box, put the box in the shopping bag.

One of the homeless walks by. We speak.

A brilliant, cold beginning, this day's sun flashes in and out of the remaining leaves of the beech and maple; the scruffy alder branches brush my arms carrying the box, a box that is heavier than I had thought a five-inch cube of ashes could be. I balance us down the hardening bank, a new slipperiness underfoot, until I reach the place where I know I will be able to kneel, linger a bit, and let my child go. I hear the early morning traffic on Main Street, the idling engines at the Dunkin Donuts drive-through. I slip the top off, lift out the bag, untwist the tie, and dump the sepia-tinged ashes into this river that will carry them to the sea, and then around the world.

I sit on a large cold boulder and watch magenta light rupture the sky. Time unfolds and undoes space.

This River

LAURIE APGAR CHANDLER

In the morning,
dancing current takes my boat, paddle touches water, and I am home.

In the afternoon,
cares relinquished to a quiet eddy, I drift on,
drowsy, dreamy river time fills the void,
thoughts come, deep as a shadowed pool, bright as sun glint.
What is this place that humbles and empowers, where I know my truest self?

In the evening,
ledge perching in the gathering quilt of darkness,
I gaze deep within the falls to pockets of sea-glass green,
and the magic of a thousand tiny cascades
becoming one, drawn by the endless force of gravity.
What is this river?
Fireflies blink an answer to the stars above.

It is water,
of course, hurtling frothy and white down a perfect set of steps,
swirling, sun-dappled, dusted-moted into the arms of a silver maple,
the flow born anew each moment, then whisked away in a breath.

It is bedrock,
cradling the waters, guiding their way,
hardened child of volcanic fury
or softer witness to the sediments of ancient oceans,
even crazy mosaics, like pebbles from some giant's sandbox,
where a single dainty purple flower
bows in the breeze.

It is the guardians,
watchful evergreens clinging to rugged cliffs through winter's icy clutch,
cow lilies, the yellow delight of moose,
and the brilliant cardinal flower, a drop of lifeblood along the grassy shore.

It is the others,
silvery leaps of faith, pulled upstream by urges strong as steel,
dark shadows that slip among the reeds on secret hidden paths,
the swooping outrage of kingfisher or pause of heron.
They know this place as I never will.

And me, and you, who yearn to understand the river's soul, and to belong.

The River Mystery

JENNIFER NELSON SIMPSON

It was the end of a typical toasty, humid summer evening along the Penobscot River. The sun had started its descent into the horizon, and colorful streaks of dusk scattered across the sky. The beaver had been sleeping in his small lodge just next to the river when a strange and frightening noise awakened him. It sounded like a waterfall splashing onto the shallow rocks of a riverbed—an odd water flow. It wasn't the normal flow of calming waters he was used to, and he didn't really know what to make of it.

Following the noise, the wary beaver crept from his refuge and peered through the tall grasses. Crickets softly chirped, and little butterflies drifted in the wind as usual. It was a tranquil, familiar scene, but something was off. The river was much lower than he was used to, making him wonder if the water could still cover the secret entrance to his dwelling. He had built this entrance underwater specifically so he would not be disturbed. His black eyes scanned the riverbank, searching for the source of the changes.

At last, he discovered some sort of strange gray mass sitting in his beautiful water. The gray thing wasn't moving. It just stood there and stared at him. It was as tall as a tree and as wide as the river, taking up a lot of space. The gray thing had sharp edges that extended into each side of the riverbank like giant arms holding onto the sides of the land. Then he saw water pouring through the gray object's large, wide mouth, spraying out from between its gaping teeth.

His mind raced with mixed thoughts and questions. *Where did all the water go? How does the gray thing hold it? Why? What is going on?*

He inched toward the gray mass, noticing his usual terrain was a little different. Brown plots now marked the ground where wildflowers, weeds, and small trees used to be. No longer could he hear bees buzz or squirrels rush about with their nuts. The beaver stood there on the bald area of brown, ugly dirt and paused to think.

He swore he had supplies here. Every day, he carefully chewed sticks and made it a point to place each one in a very specific location along the river. No stick was the same, and he'd spent a lifetime collecting them and ensuring they were properly chewed. He estimated he was missing over 200 sticks—a year's worth! The beaver looked even more closely at the riverbank. He poked at the dirt, hoping that maybe his sticks had been covered by mud, but there was nothing. His heart sank as he realized everything he had worked on was gone.

He looked to the riverbank and sighed with relief. Grasses, cattails, and watercress along the river were his favorite treats on a warm summer evening like this, and it would have been a great disappointment to him if they had disappeared. He wasn't sure what he would do without food. He hadn't thought about moving far away or trying to find a new area on the river. His entire life had been changed, and he didn't quite know what to think.

The beaver scurried closer to the large gray object and found himself blocked by a metal thing with thin gaps. It lined the area, cutting off his entry. He carefully scuttled along its edges and realized it was a fence. The beaver had heard of these before and knew they were hard to get around. He paused once he was right beside it and put his paw up to one of the spaces to see if he could crawl through. Unfortunately, the gaps were small squares, and he could only fit a paw through them.

How was he supposed to get closer to the gray item in the river? He couldn't fit through the fence holes, and looking up, he feared how high the fence towered. The barrier was as tall as a mountain, and there was no way he could climb up. Realizing he was blocked and wouldn't find out what that big gray thing was, the beaver sat down and stared at the ground in sadness.

The ground!

What an idea he had! He could dig a bit and get through the fence by going under it. He hopped over and got right to work. He picked a place under the fence that was already soft and easy to dig. With five rough claws on each paw, he grasped at the loose, heavy dirt. He dug and dug until there was a hole large enough for him to crawl through. He felt proud of what he'd done and was ready to continue on his adventure toward the gray thing.

The fence wasn't going to let him through easily, though. So he rolled onto his back and pushed his head through the hole. Next, he grabbed onto the bottom of the fence, holding on tight and pulling his plump brown body through. Then, the beaver pushed himself farther away from the fence to allow room for his big, bold tail. He usually used it to slap the water to defend himself when danger was near, but it slid perfectly through the hole. At last, he made it to the other side of the fence.

He hastened closer to the river's edge to peer at the big gray thing. It felt like it was far away, and he could not understand why this gray thing would suddenly sit in the middle of the river.

All the creatures along the river enjoyed the water with its free-flowing movement. But now that the water ran lower, the beaver would have a hard time catching fish. He wondered what would happen to the other wildlife in the area. The deer, moose, birds, fish, and even humans would have a hard time fishing. It just didn't seem right, and he wasn't sure why the water would be boxed up and held away from everyone like this.

Finally, the beaver reached the gray thing. He stepped onto it, fearing the unknown. It was cold, hard, and smooth. Yet, the gray thing did not move, and it did not acknowledge his presence. The mouths spilled water from six holes, and it seemed as though it was just a giant wall with no actual purpose. He shivered.

And then it struck him.

He was standing on a human creation he had long heard rumors about. It was something they had created to capture the water and keep it contained. The gray thing was a ... a ... a dam!

Shaking his head in disappointment, the beaver went back to his place of refuge. All he could think of was survival. With a river this low and less water running downstream for the area animals, it was going to be harder for them to survive.

He considered building another lodge farther down the river. But would another beaver find it? Would they fight him for food and water? He thought about all the hard work that was going to have to happen before winter and then thought of the other animals. What would they do? Would they leave the area? Should *he* leave the area? He worried about getting enough supplies by winter.

Reaching his lodge, he saw that the water level barely covered the entrance. But he loved his home and saw that he could make adjustments to get through winter. He wasn't going to leave or give up. Instead, the beaver began to search for sticks, forage for food, and prepare for winter.

A note to readers: Beavers create natural dams, and humans build dams made of concrete. Many human-made dams have been removed over time, but there are still more that keep wildlife from flourishing. Water is vital to all creatures, and no dam is worth the cost to our environment.

Isn't It Beautiful?

AVALON TATE

Isn't it beautiful?
The earth is spinning, the wind is blowing, the birds are singing, and
we are breathing.
We are living.
We are existing.

We are verbs.

And isn't that beautiful?

Existence is not a thing. It's an act. A dance.
You exist. You live. You breathe.
You love. You cry. You ache.
And you wish for tomorrow never to come.

The earth is spinning, oceans are rising, wars are occurring, and we
are screaming.
We are drowning.
We are dying.

We are verbs.

And isn't that terrifying?

Existence is not a thing. It's an act. A dance.

With every breath we take, we hold the power of change.
Because we breathe.
We love. We cry. We ache.
And we wish that tomorrow we'll be accepted.

The earth is dying, and we are denying it.
We need help from each other.

We are verbs.

And isn't that a mystery?

Existence is not a thing. It's an act. A dance.
Most of us cannot make the changes the world desperately needs.
But those of us who can, must.
Because we love. We cry. We ache.
And screw tomorrow. Because today we need to breathe.

Contributors

Claire Ackroyd is a landscape designer and an independent organic certification inspector. Her certification work led her to the remote sugar camps above Jackman, Maine, which became the background for her debut novel, *Murder in the Maple Woods* (Maine Authors Publishing), a finalist for the Maine Literary Award.

Doug Barrett's poetry has appeared in *Avocet* and *Canary* and is forthcoming in *Weber: The Contemporary West.* www.natureofpoetry.com

K.W. Bernard loves writing dark, violent fantasies with messy romances. She prefers rundown estates, leather, and armed scoundrels to pretty palaces, fancy dresses, and princes. A lifelong Mainer with a background in ecology, she shares the same reverence for the woods and sea as her characters.

Matt Bernier is a civil engineer for the National Marine Fisheries Service. His poetry has been published in various print and online journals, featured in the *Maine Sunday Telegram*'s "Deep Water" column and Maine Public's *Poems from Here*, and placed first in the Belfast Poetry Festival's 2023 Maine Postmark Poetry Contest.

Shannon Bowring has been nominated for the Pushcart and Best of the Net Prizes and has earned recognition via the Maine Literary Awards and the Writer's Digest Short Story Competition. Her debut novel, *The Road to Dalton* (Europa Editions), was included in the June 2023 Indie Next List. She is currently working on the sequel, *Where the Forest Meets the River*.

James Brasfield is the author of three poetry collections, his most recent *Cove* (Louisiana State University Press). He is the recipient of a National Endowment for the Arts fellowship in poetry and the PEN Award for Poetry in Translation.

Linda Buckmaster's poetry, essays, and fiction have appeared in more than forty journals. She is the author of two books, *Space Heart: A Memoir in Stages* (Burrow Press) and *Elemental: A Miscellany of Salt Cod and Islands* (Huntress Press), a finalist in the Maine Literary Awards. She is working on "Of Cod and Communities," a traveling literary exhibit.

Morgan Campbell, a licensed practical nurse, has been writing since he was ten. He is working with his mom, Valerie Campbell, to run their writing business, Wolf Prints Inc.

Valerie Campbell is an author, cover artist, licensed mental health counselor, and clinical trauma professional. She draws on her knowledge of psychology and trauma to enhance her fictional characters and has self-published the novels *Update or Die* and *Stairs to Nowhere*. Together with her son, Morgan Campbell, they run Wolf Prints Inc., a writing business. www.wolfprintbooks.com

Sarah Carlson is the author of *The Radiance of Change* (Meanderings Publications), *In the Currents of Quiet* (Meanderings Publications), and *Tender Light Softens: When the Deep Places Speak* (Golden Dragonfly Press). meanderingsoftheheart.blogspot.com

Sarah Walker Caron is a college instructor, editor, food and feature writer, and the author of eight books, including the recently released *Disney Princess Tea Parties Cookbook* (Insight Editions) and the *Super Easy 5-Ingredient Cookbook* (Rockridge Press). Her writing has appeared in the *Washington Post*, the *Boston Globe*, *Connecticut Magazine*, and *The Today Show* website. She was named columnist of the year by the Maine Press Association in 2015.

Laurie Apgar Chandler is the author of *Upwards: The Story of the First Woman to Solo Thru-Paddle the Northern Forest Canoe Trail* (Maine Authors Publishing) and *Through Woods & Waters: A Solo Journey to Maine's New National Monument* (Custom Museum Publishing). Her "View from the River" column is published monthly in the *Northwoods Sporting Journal*.

Michelle Choiniere teaches English as a second language to high schoolers. Writing poems is a new passion that she hopes to develop.

Kristen Clanton teaches English and writing at the Maine Central Institute. Nominated for the Pushcart Prize, her poetry and short fiction have been published in numerous journals, including *Arkana*, *BlazeVOX*, the *South Florida Poetry Journal*, and the *Sugar House Review*. Her first novel, *The Swallows*, was released in 2023 by Witch Way Publishing.

Loren Coleman is the author, coauthor, and contributor to over 100 books, including *Cryptozoology A to Z: The Encyclopedia of Loch Monsters, Sasquatch, Chupacabras, and Other Authentic Mysteries of Nature* (Simon & Schuster). He is also the founder and director of the nonprofit International Cryptozoology Museum in Portland and Bangor.

Ryan George Collins has written various tomes collectively known as the *Tales from the Omni Vault*, which include works like *Occult Mafia*, *Emerald of Madoc City*, and *Operation Red Dragon: The Daikaiju Wars, Part 1*.

Katie Coppens teaches science at Falmouth Middle School. She has published eight STEM-themed books for children and has won three national awards for her writing, including the Ben Franklin Award and the Nautilus Award. Since 2018, Katie has written a column for the National Science Teaching Association's *Science Scope* magazine on integrating science and literacy.

Mary Morton Cowan writes for young readers. Her river drive story was originally published in her book *Timberrr ... A History of Logging in New England* (Millbrook Press), which won the Maine Library Association Lupine Honor Award. The author of seven books, she has penned nearly 100 articles, stories, and activities for children's magazines.

Betty Culley's debut young-adult verse novel, *Three Things I Know Are True* (HarperTeen), was the 2021 Maine Literary Award winner for Young People's Literature. Her middle-grade novel, *Down to Earth* (Crown Books for Young Readers), won the Maine Library Association's Lupine Award and was a Maine Student Book Award nominee. www.bettyculley.com

Chris Davis often focuses on nostalgic stories from the area during her formative years in the 1970s and '80s. Her first solo work, *Worthy: The Memoir of an Ex-Mormon Lesbian* (Publish Your Purpose), was published in 2023. chrisdavisproud.com

Kara Douglas is a writer and yoga and meditation teacher. She has published her work in several anthologies, including *Wait: Poems from the Pandemic* (Littoral Books), *A Dangerous New World: Maine Voices on the Climate Crisis* (Littoral Books), and *From the Mountains to the Sea: The Historic Restoration of the Penobscot River* (Islandport Press).

Mo Drammeh is a University of Maine student. In 2022, he won the Crime Flash Competition from MWPA and was named one of *Maine Magazine*'s Mainers of the Year.

Kathleen Ellis is the author of several poetry collections, including *Red Horses* (Northern Lights), *Outer-Body Travel* (Finishing Line Press), and *Body of Evidence* (Grayson Books), which won the 2022 Grayson Books Poetry Contest. Her poems have appeared in *The Café Review* and the *Connecticut River Review*, as well as in the anthologies *Rumors, Secrets & Lies: Poems about Pregnancy, Abortion, & Choice* (Anhinga Press) and *A Dangerous New World: Maine Voices on the Climate Crisis* (Littoral Books).

Jean Anne Feldeisen has written for *Next Avenue* and *Chicken Soup for the Soul* and hosts the *Crows Feet: Life as We Age* podcast. Her poetry has been published in *Neologism*, *The Raven's Perch*, *The Hopper*, and *Spank the Carp*. Her first poetry chapbook, *Not All Are Weeping* (Main Street Rag), was published in 2023. jeanfeldeisen.com

Gabriella Fryer published the poetry chapbook *Muted Red* through Bottlecap Press, and her poetry has been featured in *Shemom* and the *Broadside Journal*.

Hank Garfield's first novel, *Moondog* (St. Martin's Press), was published in 1995. Since then, he has published several more books and short stories. His blog, *Slower Traffic*, details living in Maine without owning a car.

Suzanne DeWitt Hall is the author of *Where True Love Is* devotionals, the *Living in Hope* series, the *Path of Unlearning* faith deconstruction books, and the *Rumplepimple* series. Her debut novel, *The Language of Bodies* (Woodhall Press), was published in 2022.

Alice May Hotopp is a writer, ecologist, and doctoral candidate in ecology and environmental studies at the University of Maine. alicehotopp.wixsite.com/my-site

Annaliese Jakimides has published prose and poetry in many journals, magazines, and anthologies, including *Beloit Poetry Journal, GQ, Utne Reader,* and *Breaking Bread: Essays from New England on Food, Hunger, and Family* (Beacon Press), the recipient of two 2023 Maine Literary Awards. Cited in national competitions and nominated for the Pushcart and Best of the Net Prizes, her work has also been broadcast on Maine Public and NPR. Annaliese is the cowriter of the musical *Love Affair*, premiering in 2024. annaliesejakimides.com

Josh Kauppila finds their way through poverty and recovery with a steady diet of community, organizing, and occasional farm and yard work. Their poetry is mostly unpublished and happily shared for this cause.

Robert Klose teaches at the University of Maine. He is a regular contributor to the *Christian Science Monitor*. His work has also appeared in *Newsweek* and the *Boston Globe*. His books include *The Three-Legged Woman & Other Excursions in Teaching* (University Press of New England) and the novels *Long Live Grover Cleveland* (Medallion Press), which won the Ben Franklin Literary and USA Book News Awards, and *Life on Mars* (Black Rose Writing), which was a finalist in the International Book Awards. His latest novel, *Trigger Warning* (Open Books), was published in 2023.

Hans Krichels penned *We Have Met the Enemy* (Maine Authors Publishing) and *Willie Knows Who Done It* (Atmosphere Press). He has also written for various newspapers and other publications.

Elliana LaBree is an eighth grader at the Orono Middle School. At four, she was diagnosed with orbital rhabdomyosarcoma, and by age five, after extensive proton beam radiation therapy and chemotherapy, her body showed no signs of cancer. Today, Elliana enjoys playing chess, participating in dramatic theater, and playing video games.

Shane Layman graduated from the University of Maine, Orono, with a bachelor's in English/creative writing. He works as a children's librarian.

Catherine J.S. Lee is the author of two award-winning collections, *All That Remains: A Haiku Collection Inspired by a Maine Childhood* (Turtle Light Press) and *Island Secrets: Stories from the Coast of Maine* (Sea Smoke Press).

Christopher C.C. Lee is a former public school teacher and software programmer.

Paul A. Liebow, MD (1946–2021), was an emergency physician. He strongly advocated environmental responsibility and discovered his passion for writing later in life. His legacy lives on in his poetry and passionate contributions to the Maine communities he loved.

J.D. Mankowski's young-adult fantasy novel, *The Silver Scepter* (CreateSpace Independent), was published in 2015. Since then, his works have appeared in collaborative story universes and fiction anthologies.

"Twinkle" Marie Manning is a semiretired television producer, community minister, and author. Her inspirational writings have been included in publications and services around the world. www.twinklesplace.org

Meadow Rue Merrill is the award-winning author of *Redeeming Ruth: Everything Life Takes, Love Restores* (Hendrickson). She also corresponded for *The Boston Globe*, published parenting essays to the *New York Times*, and served as a contributing editor to *Down East* magazine.

Douglas W. Milliken is a queer composer, artist, and writer. He is the author of the novels *To Sleep as Animals* (Publication Studio/PS Hudson), *Our Shadows' Voice* (Fomite Press), and *Enclosure Architect* (forthcoming) and the collection *Blue of the World*. Douglas is a recipient of the Pushcart Prize and has honors from MWPA, *Glimmer Train*, and RA & Pin Drop Studios. www.douglaswmilliken.com

Sherri Mitchell Weh'na Ha'mu Kwasset is an Indigenous attorney, activist, and author from the Penobscot Nation. She is an alumna of the American Indian Ambassador Program and the Udall Native American Congressional Internship Program. Sherri is the author (with Larry Dossey) of *Sacred Instructions: Indigenous Wisdom for Living Spirit-Based Change* (North Atlantic Books) and a contributor to eleven anthologies, including the bestseller *All We Can Save: Truth, Courage, and Solutions for the Climate Crisis* (One World).

MC Moeller writes the Pyke Island Mystery series under the pen name Moe Claire. In between full-length novels, she works on short stories, community theater plays, and poetry.

Leslie Moore is the author/artist of *What Rough Beasts: Poetry/Prints* (Littoral Books) and *Grackledom: Poetry, Prints, and Drawings* (Littoral Books), and the winner of the 2018 Maine Literary Award for Short Nonfiction. Her works have been published in the *English Journal*, *The Maine Review*, *The Café Review*, *Deep Water*, and *Spire: The Maine Journal of Conservation and Sustainability*.

Pam Dixon Oertel self-published her first children's book, *Lucy Leaf*, in 2022.

Christopher Packard is a high school science teacher and the author of *Mythical Creatures of Maine: Fantastic Beasts from Legend and Folklore* (Down East Books) and the children's book *Lumpy's Gift* (12 Willows Press).

lisa panepinto is the author of *where i come from the fish have souls* (Spuyten Duyvil) and *On This Borrowed Bike* (Three Rooms Press).

Gary Rainford has written three poetry collections—*Salty Liquor* (North Country Press), *Liner Notes* (North Country Press), and *Adrift* (North Country Press)—and was a 2022 finalist for the Independent Publishers of New England Poetry Award. www.garyrainford.com

Patricia Smith Ranzoni is the poet laureate for Bucksport. Her writing can be found in the *Maine Arts Journal*, *Still Mill: Poems, Stories & Songs of Making Paper*, and *Tellus/Ecopoesia* (Italy).

Rhea Côté Robbins has published the memoirs *'down the Plains'* (Rheta Press) and *Wednesday's Child* (Rheta Press), a winner of the Maine Writers & Publishers Alliance's (MWPA) Creative Nonfiction Chapbook Award. She edited *Canuck and Other Stories* (Rheta Press), an anthology of translations of early twentieth-century Franco-American women writers. She also edited the anthology *Heliotrope: French Heritage Women Create* (Rheta Press), a finalist in MWPA's anthology competition. Rhea's poetry has been published in several literary journals and anthologies.

Emma G. Rose is an author, podcast host, and publisher. She founded Imperative Press to publish her first novel, *Nothing's Ever Lost*. Now with four books in print, she's the cohost of the *Indie Book Talk* podcast.

Lee Sands lives with their family in Maine along the Penobscot, where they enjoy the four seasons reflected by our jewel state.

Catherine Schmitt has penned three books: *The President's Salmon: Restoring the King of Fish and Its Home Waters* (Down East Books), *Historic Acadia National Park* (Lyons Press), and *A Coastal Companion: A Year in the Gulf of Maine from Cape Cod to Canada* (Tilbury House). catherineschmitt.com

Michelle E. Shores wrote *Vital Records of Bangor, Maine*, Volumes 1 and 2 (Picton Press). In 2022 she published *The Gathering Room: A Tale of Nelly Butler* (Maine Authors Publishing), the winner of the Independent Publishers Book Awards Bronze Medal for Best Fiction in the Northeast Region and a National Indie Excellence Award Finalist for Best Historical Fiction.

Jennifer Nelson Simpson lives in Bangor with her family and pets.

Brenda E. Smith published the memoir *Becoming Fearless: Finding Courage in the African Wilderness* (Eye Opener Press) in 2023. www.eyeopenerpress.com

Karin Spitfire won national first place in the 2019 Joe Gouveia Outermost Poetry Contest for "Liquidation." The author of *The Body in Late Stage Capitalism* (Illuminated Sea Press), *Standing with Trees* (Illuminated Sea Press), and the chapbook *Wild Caught*, her poems have appeared in *Canary: A Literary Journal of the Environmental Crisis*, *The Catch Trivia: Voices of Feminism*, and *Currents: The Journal of Body Mind Centering Association*. She was the poet laureate for Belfast in 2007 and 2008.

Ret Talbot is an award-winning independent journalist, science writer, and author. His most recent book is *Chasing Shadows* (William Morrow), written with the shark biologist Greg Skomal. Ret's work appears in publications like *Discover Magazine*, *National Geographic*, and *Yale Environment 360,* and he frequently lectures at secondary schools and colleges/universities about his research and writing.

Avalon Tate is an eighth-grade student at Beech Hill School. "Isn't It Beautiful?" is the 2023 Telling Room Statewide Writing Contest winner for Hancock County.

Meg Weston is the cofounder of The Poets Corner and the Camden Festival of Poetry. The author of the poetry collection *Magma Intrusions* (Kelsay Books), her work has appeared in several journals and anthologies, including the *Hawaii Pacific Review, The Trouvaille Review*, *Red Fez*, and *The Mountain Troubadour*. www.volcanoes.com

Geoff Wingard is a writer and teacher. His previously published work includes curricula for the National Endowment for the Humanities, the Newark Museum, the Maine Folklife Center, and other educational institutions. He has also written on social history, the martial arts, and speculative fiction set in near-future Maine.

Printed in the USA
CPSIA information can be obtained
at www.ICGtesting.com
LVHW052330110124
768815LV00039B/879